"What makes you so damn sure you've got what I'm looking for?" Wolfe demanded.

"I didn't say that," Storm murmured, her long lashes dropping to veil her eyes.

"You've been saying it all day. What's wrong, Storm, didn't you think I'd get curious?"

Her dark lashes rose and her eyes were definitely laughing. "Now, don't do anything you'll regret later. We both know I've goaded you into this, and if you let me get away with it . . . I'll always know which buttons to push."

He'd been tantalized by her all evening, attracted and irritated, amused and angered, fascinated and defensive. Even with all his inner alarms jangling, he simply couldn't be sensible about her.

"I know I'm going to regret this," he said, then pulled her into his arms. What he felt in those first moments was not regret. It was like a detonation, an explosion of sensation so intense, it jarred his body and shocked his mind. Her mouth was alive under his, and there was so much heat between them, he knew they were both going to get burned . . . .

WHAT ARE *LOVESWEPT* ROMANCES?

They are stories of true romance and touching emotion. We believe those two very important ingredients are constants in our highly sensual and very believable stories in the *LOVESWEPT* line. Our goal is to give you, the reader, stories of consistently high quality that may sometimes make you laugh, sometimes make you cry, but are always fresh and creative and contain many delightful surprises within their pages.

Most romance fans read an enormous number of books. Those they truly love, they keep. Others may be traded with friends and soon forgotten. We hope that each *LOVESWEPT* romance will be a treasure—a "keeper." We will always try to publish

*LOVE STORIES YOU'LL NEVER FORGET
BY AUTHORS YOU'LL ALWAYS REMEMBER*

The Editors

Loveswept® 607

Men of Mysteries Past

Kay Hooper
Hunting the Wolfe

BANTAM BOOKS

NEW YORK · TORONTO · LONDON · SYDNEY · AUCKLAND

HUNTING THE WOLFE

A Bantam Book / April 1993

LOVESWEPT and the wave design are registered trademarks of Bantam Books, a division of Bantam Doubleday Dell Publishing Group, Inc. Registered in U.S. Patent and Trademark Office and elsewhere.

All rights reserved.
Copyright © 1993 by Kay Hooper.
Cover art copyright © 1993 by Lina Levy.
No part of this book may be reproduced or transmitted in any form or by any means, electronic or mechanical, including photocopying, recording, or by any information storage and retrieval system, without permission in writing from the publisher.
For information address: Bantam Books.

If you purchased this book without a cover, you should be aware that this book is stolen property. It was reported as "unsold and destroyed" to the publisher, and neither the author nor the publisher has received any payment for this "stripped book."

If you would be interested in receiving protective vinyl covers for your Loveswept books, please write to this address for information:

Loveswept
Bantam Books
P.O. Box 985
Hicksville, NY 11802

ISBN 0-553-44374-7

Published simultaneously in the United States and Canada

Bantam Books are published by Bantam Books, a division of Bantam Doubleday Dell Publishing Group, Inc. Its trademark, consisting of the words "Bantam Books" and the portrayal of a rooster, is Registered in U.S. Patent and Trademark Office and in other countries. Marca Registrada. Bantam Books, 666 Fifth Avenue, New York, New York 10103.

PRINTED IN THE UNITED STATES OF AMERICA

OPM   0 9 8 7 6 5 4 3 2 1

Great things are done when men and mountains meet.

—WILLAM BLAKE

There is a passion for hunting something deeply implanted in the human breast.
—CHARLES DICKENS

One

When Wolfe Nickerson stalked into the museum's computer room in the middle of a Tuesday afternoon, one look at his face should have warned anyone that he was not in a good mood. Unfortunately the computer technician who was kneeling half under the main desk couldn't see his face. So his brusque voice and somewhat imperious summons caused her to bump her head—hard—against the underside of the desk.

"Hey you," he growled, snapping his fingers as he looked around the room that was filled with various machines, monitors, and control panels.

He heard the thud, and it drew his attention to the desk. Then he saw the top of a rather wild blond head being rubbed by one small hand, and a pair of fierce green eyes glaring up at him.

In a voice that was every bit as intense as her eyes and held a strong Southern accent, she said, "To summon a cab you can snap your fingers. To call a forgiving dog you can snap your fingers. But if you want a printable response from *me*, use my name."

"I don't know your name," he retorted.

She let out a little sigh of aggravation and climbed to her feet, still rubbing her head. Her expression remained somewhat annoyed, though her voice was milder. "That is true, but hardly an excuse. You might at least have said 'Hey, lady,' or 'Excuse me, miss.'"

"I didn't know you were a—woman," Wolfe said. He realized he was being stared at, and decided he'd better clarify that statement. "I mean, I wasn't aware that Ace would be sending me a female technician. And I couldn't see you when I came into the room."

"Next time," she said, "knock."

For a little thing she certainly had an attitude, he thought. He towered over her by nearly a foot, but she was obviously not in the least intimidated. In fact, there was something slightly mocking in her expression. Wolfe wasn't used to being treated with mockery, especially by a woman.

"What is your name?" he demanded.

"Storm Tremaine."

He didn't immediately respond to the information, even though he'd asked for it. He wasn't often caught off guard by a person or a situation, but this was one of the rare occasions. When Ace Security had promised to send him their very best computer technician to replace the first one—who had unintentionally sabotaged the museum's new security system a couple of weeks previously—Wolfe had expected another earnest young man whose language was so technical it hardly resembled English and who probably had no interest in anything except his computers.

What Wolfe had definitely *not* expected was a pint-sized blonde somewhere in her twenties with very long and definitely wild hair, big eyes so haughty, fierce, and green any cat would have been proud to claim them, and a small but lively face that wasn't exactly pretty but certainly wouldn't be easily forgotten.

She might have been two or three inches over five feet tall if she stretched her neck a bit and stood up very straight. And she might have weighed a hundred pounds, but he thought a good five **pounds** of that would probably be the hair. There was an awful lot of the stuff, bright gold and untamed, hanging in loose curls past her waist. She was very small, her bones delicate, and there was not an ounce of excess flesh anywhere that he could see. Since she was wearing an oversized sweater over jeans, he couldn't begin to guess at her measurements, but all that wild hair was the essence of femininity.

Wolfe had a thing about blondes, but he preferred them tall, sleek, and leggy. This one hardly fit the mold. In fact, judging by what he'd seen of her temperament, her hair should have been red. He was almost certain it was meant to be red.

He eyed her, not entirely pleased because she certainly didn't look like his mental image of a crackerjack computer technician. "Your name is Storm?" he asked dryly.

She returned the stare, then put small hands on her hips and, with a total lack of self-consciousness, looked him up and down slowly and thoroughly, missing nothing along the way. "Well, as I understand it, yours is Wolfe. So let's not cast stones, huh?"

There was too much justice in that for him to be able to take exception to it, but he was definitely annoyed by her attitude. "Look, in case nobody told you—you work for me."

Without hesitation and in a very matter-of-fact way, she said, "My job is to complete the installation of a computerized security system in this museum. I work for Ace Security first because they are my employers, Max Bannister second because he hired us to do a job, and the San Francisco Museum of Historical Art third because the job is here. Fourth is Morgan West, who is the director of the *Mysteries Past* exhibit. You come in fifth, since being head of security for the exhibit is a narrow area of responsibility. And since Mr. Bannister is away—I believe on his honeymoon—I answer directly to you on any problems concerning security."

She smiled. "And I don't need any of you hovering over me. In case nobody told *you*—I'm very good at what I do."

"That remains to be seen," Wolfe said. He felt very irritated at her but, at the same time, couldn't take his eyes off her vividly expressive face. It was a disconcerting combination of reactions.

She nodded slightly, clearly accepting his challenge. "Fair enough. I'll be quite happy to prove myself. I'll work, and work hard, but, as I said, not with you standing there glowering at me. To coin a phrase, this room's too small for the both of us. Was there a reason you came in here?"

"Yes, there was a reason." He knew he sounded as annoyed as he felt. "I wanted to know how long the door alarms will be deactivated. I need the guards stationed in the corridors while the museum's open, not on the doors."

Storm sat down in the swivel chair behind the desk, leaned back, and propped her feet up on the desk. She was wearing very small, very scuffed western boots with high heels.

She *was* little, Wolfe realized, noting that the heels had given her at least three inches of height.

"The door alarms are back on-line," she said. "I had to take them off-line for half an hour because somebody had screwed up and mismatched four different cables, which was threatening to blow the whole system."

"It wasn't me," he heard himself say, aware of a peculiar urge to defend himself because of the way she was looking at him. At the same time he was relieved to know that she'd had a good reason for being underneath the desk. That had bothered him vaguely.

Storm laced her fingers together across her middle, still looking at him. After a moment she said mildly, "Well, it hardly matters since I fixed it. Anyway, the door alarms will remain on-line until the changeover to the new system."

"Which will be . . . ?"

"I had to wipe the hard disk and start over, so all the data has to be reentered. It'll take some time. A week. Ten days at the most."

Wolfe felt his eyebrows climbing. If she could get the new security system on-line in ten days or less, they would actually end up ahead of their original schedule. Skeptical by nature, he said, "Aren't you being optimistic about that?"

"No."

Totally against his will, he felt a flicker of amusement, and his interest in her grew. She might be little, but there was certainly nothing small about Storm Tremaine's self-confidence. It was a trait he tended to respect. "Then don't you think you'd better get started?" he suggested dryly.

She nodded toward the main computer terminal atop the desk to the right of her boots. The screen was dark, but the drive system was humming quietly. "I have started. Until the operating system finishes loading, that thing's nothing more than a very stupid, very expensive piece of junk waiting for somebody to tell it what to do. I had to start all over, remember?"

Wolfe wasn't exactly computer illiterate, but like most people he just automatically assumed the machine wasn't on if the screen was dark. Before he could either admit his ignorance or come up with a face-saving response, she tossed the subject into the limbo of unimportant things.

"How fast can you run?"

He blinked. "What?"

"Run. The mile, for instance. How fast can you run the mile?"

"About average, I suppose."

She smiled. It suddenly made him *extremely* nervous. "That's good," she said.

Warily he asked, "Why is that good?"

"I was state champ in college."

Wolfe wasn't vain enough to assume instantly that Storm had in mind a sexual pursuit, but he couldn't think of any other reason she'd be comparing their running abilities. His immediate response to the idea was definite interest—so much so that it bothered him.

Despite being a blonde, she wasn't at all his type—so why did he feel this unnervingly strong attraction to her? Was it her voice? Granted, he liked the drawling accent, but he couldn't recall ever being attracted to a woman just because of her voice. It was obvious she had a sharp mind to go along with her attitude, but he wasn't sure if that particular trait attracted him or irritated him. And if her green eyes were intriguingly unusual in their brightness and clarity, they also warned of a spirit too tempestuous to be anything but trouble for a man who disliked complications in his personal life.

So Wolfe decided to ignore the attraction. The decision was very clear and logical in his mind, so he didn't much like the pang of regret he felt. But that was probably why he couldn't just let the whole thing go, even though he rationalized it. He told himself he was interested only because he'd never heard an approach quite like hers, and he was naturally curious to find out just how far she meant to go.

That was all it was, of course.

"Are we going to be running somewhere?" he asked.

"That," she said, "depends on you."

"Storm—you don't mind if I call you Storm, do you?" His voice was very polite.

Hers was equally so. "Certainly not. After all, we're both a force of nature—Wolfe."

He crossed his arms over his chest and gazed down at her with what he hoped was an unreadable expression. His curiosity had gotten him into trouble in the past, but he was sure he could handle this diminutive blonde. Without commenting on the comparison of their names, he said, "Storm, are you implying that you'd like to mix business with pleasure?"

"Oh, no, I'd much rather keep the two separate. My business hours—like the museum's—are nine to six. During those hours I fully intend to work. But that leaves a lot of time, and I understand San Francisco has a wonderful nightlife. I don't need much sleep. How about you?"

As he gazed at her vivid face and bright eyes, Wolfe had the sudden wary feeling that there was an underlying guile in her voice or manner that he was missing, and that his instincts were trying to warn him to look beneath the surface. But what she was saying kept getting in the way.

"Somehow I don't think we'd suit each other," he said finally.

"Why?" she drawled. "Because I'm not five-foot-nine and sleek? You should widen your horizons. To say nothing of your standards."

In a voice that had more than once been termed dangerous, Wolfe said, "I'm going to strangle Morgan." Morgan West was an amused observer of his . . . socializing.

"Oh, don't blame her. She wasn't the first person who told me about your obsession with Barbie dolls. That's the worst-kept secret in the city, especially since you change them about as often as you change your socks."

He realized his teeth were gritted only because his jaw began to ache. He didn't like feeling on the defensive; it was an unusual and very uncomfortable sensation. Consciously relaxing taut muscles, he said, "Well, we all have our preferences, don't we?"

"That's put me in my place," she said, not noticeably discouraged. "Most women would view that as a rejection. I'm not most women. And I really do think you owe it to yourself to at least give me a try."

"Why?" he demanded bluntly. He could have sworn there was a fleeting gleam of laughter in her cat's eyes, but her slightly drawling voice remained almost insultingly dispassionate.

"Because a steady diet of *anything* is going to taste awfully bland eventually. If it must be blondes, the least you can do is broaden the range a bit to include those of us who aren't tall even on a stepladder and who don't have blue eyes—which are very common, by the way. Why not put a little spice in your life? I can guarantee you won't be bored."

Before he could stop himself, Wolfe retorted, "That's not what I'm worried about."

A little laugh escaped her. "Afraid I'd cling and be demanding? Happily ever after and a white picket fence? Well, I don't cling, and I tend to ask rather than demand, but as for the rest, I wouldn't rule it out. In fact, small-town Southern girls have that goal drummed into them practically from birth. But I could hardly drag you to the altar bound and gagged, now, could I? And since you're captain of your fate and master of your soul—to say nothing of being considerably larger than me—I imagine it wouldn't do me much good to catch you. Unless you wanted to be caught, that is."

Wolfe had another uneasy feeling, this time that his mouth was open. He was thirty-six, which meant that his interest in females—and vice versa—went back more than twenty years. If he'd wanted, he could have told some colorful stories; he was a scarred veteran of the romantic wars. But this was a first for him.

Was she simply a very honest woman? A woman who was attracted to a man she'd just met and said so without hesitation or any attempt to play games? Somehow he wasn't quite prepared to buy that. He wasn't that vain—or that gullible. And he was a skeptical man.

Even acknowledging the attraction he felt and assuming she felt the same pull toward him, it didn't automatically follow that the sparks were positive ones. In fact, their reactions to each other had so far been more sharp and testy than libidinous. And even discounting that, the few minutes they'd spent together hardly encouraged either one of them to assume they'd have anything at all in common.

So . . . what was she up to?

He frowned down at her, trying to listen to his instincts. "I'm getting a little confused. Are you after a date, a lover, or a husband?"

"Well, that depends on your stamina, doesn't it? At least I assume that's your problem. Judging by what I know of your track record, there must be *some* reason why you haven't been able to go the distance—any distance at all, in fact—with any of your previous blondes."

Whatever Wolfe's instincts were trying to tell him was drowned in the roar of his temper. Biting every word off, he said, "Did it ever occur to you that the *problem* might simply be a lack of continuing interest on both sides?"

Storm pursed her lips thoughtfully. "I suppose it might have occurred to me, but I figure that any man who dates only carbon copies of one type of woman must be sure that he knows what he wants, and certainly should know what makes him happy. Assuming that, you must be satisfied with brief, surface relationships—or else you'd make an effort to try something different. Ergo, if there is a problem . . . it's yours."

Wolfe didn't really follow the logic of her argument, mostly because her drawling voice and dispassionate tone—not to mention her words—were feeding his temper steadily. If she'd set out to make him so mad he would act purely on impulse, she couldn't have done a better job.

Almost growling the question, he asked, "Did you drive here this morning?"

"No, I took a cab."

"Then meet me out front at six."

"You're on," she said promptly.

Wolfe turned on his heel and stalked from the room.

After a few moments Storm took her boots off the desk and got up. She went to the door and closed it quietly. She leaned against it, gazing at nothing in particular, until a beep from the computer terminal drew her back to the desk. Returning to her chair, she removed a floppy disk from the computer's drive slot and replaced it with another she took from a disk file beside the keyboard. She typed a short command, and the computer began humming softly once again.

Her actions were automatic and unthinking, and during most of the process she gazed absently toward the door. Finally, however, she leaned back in her chair and peered under the desk.

"Why didn't you come out and provide a little distraction?" she asked in a chiding tone. "It might have saved me from the consequences of my own insanity."

"Yaah," her companion answered in a voice so soft it was hardly a murmur, and came out from under the desk to jump on top of it.

The cat was an almost eerie feline replication of Storm. It was very small and appeared delicate; its thick and rather wavy fur was the exact same shade of pale gold as her hair; and its eyes were a vibrant green. Even the small face held the same vividness that was in Storm's expression.

A very superstitious, slightly drunk man had once—fleetingly—believed that Storm had actually turned herself into a cat. And a good thing, too; his brief moment of alcohol-induced terror had given her the opportunity she'd needed to escape.

Shrugging off that memory, Storm eyed her cat reprovingly. "Don't tell me he scared you."

The cat began to wash a blond forepaw with studied disinterest.

"Yeah, right," Storm said. "Bear, you're almost as good a liar as I am." She frowned slightly. "He's a wolf, you're a bear, and I'm a storm. If any more feral names pop up, I'm going home. It wouldn't exactly be a good omen."

"Yaahh," Bear replied, sounding, as always, the way he looked—like a very small and very meek kitten rather than a full-grown cat who had turned five on his last birthday.

Since Storm's work often kept her in small rooms filled with quiet machinery for hours at a time, and since there were long stretches during which there was nothing for her to do except wait for a computer to finish digesting whatever information she'd been feeding it, she had grown into the habit of talking to her cat. Bear had been her constant companion ever since he had turned up on her doorstep one rainy night five years before, a sodden, miserable, and half-starved kitten so tiny he could curl up easily in the palm of her hand.

He'd grown since then. Not much, but some.

"You might have stopped me," she said to the small, blond cat. "Distracted him, like I said. But did you? No. You just let me jump in the deep end."

Bear tilted his head to one side and uttered a soft chirp that sounded questioning.

Storm propped her elbows on the desk and sighed. "I don't know why I did it. I suppose I just wanted to bait a trap so obvious he'd run wildly in any direction except this one. And if I'd stopped with that, it sure would have kept him out from underfoot."

Bear chirped again, still questioning.

"Well, because . . ." Storm's voice trailed into silence. She really didn't want to say it aloud, even to her faithful companion. She didn't want to say that what had begun as a ruse to keep a sharp-eyed man as far away from her as possible had turned into something else, something that had left her feeling unsettled—not in the least because of what she'd begun.

Mixing business with pleasure . . . His question had been more apt than he knew. It wasn't something she was accustomed to doing, mostly because, in her business especially, it was extremely stupid. Storm was a lot of things, but stupid wasn't one of them.

But judging by the result, her brain hadn't been in command this time. Because, instead of showing just enough grasping interest to send Wolfe Nickerson fleeing as any self-preserving male should, she had deliberately goaded and provoked him until sheer temper had compelled him to take up her challenge.

The question was . . . why had she done it?

Bear made the same soft cooing sound he used when he was intent on luring an unwary bird, and it drew Storm's attention back to him.

Looking severely at the cat, she said, "I'll bet he thinks I'm the most shameless hussy west of the Mississippi, Bear. And it's not like I could blame him for thinking that. I certainly made it plain I was after his—scalp, didn't I?"

"Yah," Bear said.

Storm chewed on her bottom lip. "Okay . . . But that doesn't necessarily mean anything's going to happen, right? I made him mad just now, and once he cools down he'll remind himself that I'm really not his type—in spite of being a blonde. In fact, he'll probably convince himself I'm a bottle blonde. And . . . he'll stay out of my path from then on. Right?"

Bear blinked at her.

"You could agree just to make me feel better," Storm observed wryly. When the little cat remained silent, she sighed and pushed up the sleeve of her sweater to look at the large masculine watch on her wrist. It was one of those go-anywhere-even-to-the-bottom-of-the-ocean watches with every time zone in the world as well as a few other creative bells and whistles, and it dwarfed her delicate wrist.

She checked two time zones, did a brief mental calculation, and muttered, "Jet lag," in a faintly relieved tone.

That would certainly explain her unusual recklessness, she decided. She was just tired, that was all. She had arrived in San Francisco very late the previous night and hadn't gotten very much sleep—and her inner clock was still on Paris time.

The computer beeped again, and she automatically replaced the floppy disk with another; they were clearly numbered in the file, one through thirty, and she had just slid number ten into the machine. Holding the disk she'd removed, she slid it slowly into its sleeve and then replaced it in the file, tilted forward so that she wouldn't forget that the information on it had already been loaded into the machine.

Storm reached over to turn on the computer's monitor, and when the screen flickered to life, she studied the information scrolling briskly. Another computer technician might have noticed two things about that information. One, there was a fairly basic operating system loading on the computer's hard disk, and two, there were several command paths that didn't belong in an operating system when the program was going to be security.

Wolfe might possibly have noticed that, if he'd gotten a look at the screen. In fact, Storm was reasonably sure he would have noticed. He was not a computer expert, but his own work dealt with security, and she had no doubt that he had worked with enough computerized security systems to be able to spot open doors and other unsecured access points—even buried within cryptic mathematical formulas.

Storm didn't like to think of what he would have done if he'd seen, but she had an idea that his reaction would have resulted in her being locked away for a goodly number of years.

Or maybe not, she thought, cheering slightly. She hadn't *done* anything, after all. Nothing had been stolen. And if she'd made certain there was a backdoor into a supposedly secure system, well, that wasn't *really* illegal, was it? It was sort of an unwritten law among programmers that whoever wrote the program had a right to get in and use the thing later no matter how many access codes and locks had been put in place. And it *was* her program she'd be loading; she'd written half a dozen security programs in the last ten years, at least half of which were perfect for large-scale operations such as museums.

Which really meant the museum—as well as Maxim Bannister and his exhibit—was getting a state-of-the-art security system that had never been offered to anyone else anywhere in the world, and for which no diagrams existed anywhere—except in Storm's head. Which meant it was as secure from outside tampering as any computer system could possibly be. She had modified the operating system as well; it was a fairly standard system, necessary to run the hardware, but it was now capable of a few tricks its designers had never intended.

Storm wasn't certain she'd need those tricks, but it never hurt to be prepared. They, like the backdoor that would give her access no matter what, were simply her prerogatives as the programmer in charge of the system's design.

But Wolfe, not being a programmer, might not see it that way. Storm thought of those sharp blue eyes, and sighed. "This whole thing could get hellishly tangled," she told her cat ruefully. "And I think I made it worse. Why didn't I just take my chances that he wouldn't demand to see what I was loading? Why did I have to make a verbal pass at the man?"

Bear chirped softly and at length.

Though she didn't think about it very much, Storm was convinced that she and her cat communicated on the same level. She had even once thought that she and Bear really were two versions of the same being—one human, one feline—and that was why they understood each other so well. In any case, she often heard from Bear—or attributed to him—the balancing voice of reason she sometimes needed.

Like now.

When the cat had finished talking to her, she felt very uneasy. "I don't even like him," she objected, trying to forget her own conflicting reactions to Wolfe. "He irritated me. It was plain what kind of man he is. Even if I hadn't already heard about his fixation on blondes, I wouldn't have liked him. I'll bet he's given to long, brooding silences, and with that red in his hair he's bound to have a hell of a temper. And he's too good-looking. He's like his namesake, dammit. You can pull him in out of the wild, and you might even fool yourself into thinking you've got him domesticated, but he'll always be basically untamed. Any woman would need her head examined for thinking . . ."

"Pprrrpp?" Bear chirped softly.

The computer beeped then, offering Storm a welcome distraction. She changed floppy disks, then got up and began moving around the room checking various connections and cables. "Never mind," she said to her cat. "After tonight he'll stay away from me anyway. I'll make sure of that."

The cat didn't respond, but she could almost hear his chirping query as if he'd asked, and in English.

If she was so sure she didn't like Wolfe, and so certain she could keep him away from her, then why didn't she sound happier about it?

Storm was a bit late in leaving the museum, mostly because she'd wanted to finish loading the operating system so as to be ready for the other programs first thing next morning. As a result, she didn't lock the door of the computer room until half past six and found one of the security guards waiting for her at the front door.

"The boss said to wait and let you out," the man said.

She paused to regard him thoughtfully. "Which boss?"

"Ma'am?"

"I'm trying to figure out who runs things around here. So, which boss told you to wait for me?"

"Oh. Well—Mr. Nickerson. He's in charge of security."

Storm found the response interesting. Technically Wolfe was not, in fact, in charge of security for the *museum*, only the *Mysteries Past* exhibit. Which wasn't even in place yet. However, it was natural he would be concerned with the museum's security, since the building would house the exhibit. What Storm found interesting was the fact that the guards—and not just this man, because she'd asked a couple of others as well—really did consider Wolfe's word law.

To Storm's mind, what that said was that Wolfe had a very strong personality and was a natural leader. It also told her that in any emergency situation, it would be Wolfe the guards would look to, no matter who else was present.

Thoughtful, she nodded to the guard and passed through the door when he opened it for her. She paused just outside at the top of the wide steps, looking down toward the curb.

He was waiting for her, leaning against the hood of a late-model sports car that was, she knew, a rental. He was wearing a black leather jacket over dark slacks and a light-colored shirt, giving him a dangerous air. He was the kind of man that people would always notice. Especially women. It wasn't really the way he looked, although he was certainly handsome; it was more his bearing, just the way he stood and moved. There was a very focused quality about him, an inner certainty of himself that was more than confidence and less than ego.

He was an intriguing man, Storm had to admit—if only to herself. She was more than ever convinced that he, like his namesake, would be a very, very dangerous creature if he were cornered or otherwise threatened.

Like him, the car he leaned back against looked a little menacing. It was obviously powerful, and the gleaming black body was low slung, an almost visible growl. It would require careful handling.

Like him.

Storm tried not to think about that as she started down the steps toward him. Instead she thought about the fact that both he and she were visitors to this city, both living transient lives here. Wolfe had a sublet apartment, she knew; he was set to be here for months while the Bannister collection

18 • KAY HOOPER

of artworks and gems was being exhibited at the museum. She, on the other hand, was scheduled to be in San Francisco only a matter of a few weeks, just long enough to get the security system on-line and functioning properly; her temporary home here was a small suite in a nearby hotel.

Storm hadn't been granted a lot of time to check out the situation here before she arrived—which was her habit—because she'd gotten her orders on fairly short notice. But she was a resourceful woman, and she'd managed to find out quite a lot, certainly more than Wolfe had realized; she'd been most interested in checking him out, since he was head of security. She had found out that the two of them had some things in common—and a number of differences.

Wolfe, a security expert for Lloyd's of London, was based in New York and London; the only place she'd lived for more than a few weeks at a time during the past ten years was Paris, so if she had a base, that was probably it. So they were both accustomed to living out of a suitcase.

She wasn't attracted to any one type of man when it came to physical characteristics, but did tend to be drawn to men who were intelligent and were experts in their field.

Wolfe had a thing about blondes. That was true enough, and she'd goaded him about it but she hadn't mentioned one very important point about his seeming fixation. All the blondes he'd dated—for want of a better word—since arriving in San Francisco were in some way involved with foundations, trusts, charities, art societies, museums, or private collections of artworks, gems, and other valuables.

Smart man, she had realized with an inner salute of respect when that pattern had become apparent to her. *He* was mixing business and pleasure quite effectively, enjoying the company of his blondes while he picked their brains. In the past months he'd been in and out of San Francisco, and particularly in recent weeks when he'd been living here, he had undoubtedly gathered an impressive amount of intelligence about the close-knit art world in this city—to say nothing of having fun while he did it.

Storm respected that, and she didn't consider it a cold-blooded thing for him to do. She had once or twice dated a man purely because he could tell her something she wanted to know, so why shouldn't Wolfe? Even if he did take the matter to extremes. He was a very attractive man, obviously with a strong sex drive, who simply looked for his women where their knowledge could help him do his job most effectively.

In fact, she didn't doubt that by now Wolfe had reminded himself of her computer expertise and had come to the conclusion that he might gain some useful knowledge from her even if the first date ended up being the only one.

That also didn't bother Storm; he wasn't likely to waste his charm on her, considering the friction between them, so she wasn't worried about telling him anything she didn't want him to know. What *did* bother her was the unusual conflict she felt in her own emotions.

As much as she wanted to deny it, she felt an unnervingly strong attraction to Wolfe Nickerson— and she hadn't convinced herself that it was only jet lag. The truth was, the man had a strong effect on her, and she didn't know where that was headed. Given his track record, of course, the odds were that any relationship he began would end in the bedroom—and probably for no more than a few brief hours.

Storm wasn't a vain woman, but she was sure of herself, and she knew herself well; there was no way on earth she would ever become one of Wolfe's blondes, here today and gone tomorrow. She'd fight that with all the violence of her name, even if she had to fight him, and even if she had to use some kind of deception as a weapon.

In a way it was a challenge, and nobody had ever called her timid about picking up a gauntlet. But the growing strength of her own feelings . . . That would have disturbed her at any time, since she also knew herself well enough to know that romance in her life would be a difficult and potentially painful complication. But it especially bothered her now.

This was not a good time for her to lose her head. And Wolfe, she was certain, was not the kind of man a woman should ever, *ever* lose her head over.

Two

"Nice car," she said when she reached the curb. "But how come men drive either trucks or sports cars?"

"Max drives a Mercedes," Wolfe said, because it was the first thing that popped into his mind.

"Mercedes don't count. They're not cars, but works of art. And, anyway, I was asking you personally. So why are you driving something that looks like it belongs in a cage?"

Wolfe had spent quite a bit of time reasoning with himself during the past couple of hours, coming to the conclusion that Storm Tremaine was not only not his type, she was also virtually guaranteed to make his life far more difficult than it needed to be. He had, therefore, very calmly and rationally decided that he was not going to let her get to him during this, their first and last date.

But when he heard that drawling voice laced with mockery and looked into that small, vivid face, he could feel the irritated fascination creeping over him again. He didn't like the feeling one bit, but he couldn't seem to control it.

He also didn't have a good answer for her question. So, in the time-honored tradition, he replied with one of his own. "What do you drive?"

"Something practical," she answered promptly. "While I'm here I'll probably rent a Jeep."

He eyed her. "So you're a practical woman?" He

expected her to bristle a bit, or at least instantly deny the horrible accusation; in his experience, no woman wanted to be termed practical. But Storm—and not for the first time—didn't react as expected.

"Oh, it's far worse than that," she said in a solemn voice. "I'm a logical woman."

Wolfe had the notion that he was being warned. "So I should act accordingly?"

Storm shrugged slightly. "That's up to you. Just don't expect *me* to act like one of your Barbie dolls."

"Will you stop calling them that?"

"Are you offended on their behalf . . . or yours?"

The question brought him up short, because he realized that he *was* offended on his own behalf. That was a sobering realization, so he was naturally annoyed at Storm for having made him face it. "Look," he began, but then broke off abruptly when he noticed something odd.

There was a creature on her shoulder. He wasn't sure what it was, but it had green eyes. That was all he could see, since her hair was so thick and whatever was there blended right in.

"What is that?" he asked cautiously.

She didn't need the question clarified. With a practiced gesture she reached up and flipped her long hair behind that shoulder, revealing a very small blond cat.

"I hope you're not allergic," she said. "Bear goes everywhere with me—except into restaurants, of course."

"Bear?"

"Yes, Bear. He's my familiar."

Wolfe had an odd feeling that she wasn't kidding. And since the little cat looked eerily like her, even to the striking vividness of green eyes, the idea that there could be something supernatural between the woman and her cat didn't seem as farfetched as it should have.

"I see," he murmured.

"I doubt it."

He straightened away from the car and stared down at her, instinctively attempting a very old intimidation ploy by making his greater size obvious—and consciously aware that it wasn't working on Storm. Though her chin rose slightly when he loomed over her, she didn't step back and looked, if anything, amused rather than dismayed.

Wolfe nearly snapped the words. "Are you this confrontational with everybody, or is it just me?"

"Lots of people, but not everyone. It must be your lucky day." She smiled. "I forgot to mention. I was also captain of the debate team in college."

Wonderful, Wolfe thought with a reluctant flicker of humor. As a track star she could chase him down, and once she caught him he was never going to win an argument with her.

"This just gets better by the minute," he told her ironically.

"Oh, be brave," she said. "Surely you're not worried about one measly date. Is that why you ordered me to meet you out here, by the way? I mean, are we going somewhere? And, if so, could we get started? In case you hadn't noticed, it's a little chilly out here."

"I know I'm going to regret this." Wolfe opened the car door for her and gestured for her to get in.

"Are you a gentleman born, or is it something you have to work at?"

"Get in the car," he said.

She grinned at him and got in.

By the time Wolfe had closed her door with exquisite care and had gone around to his side, he'd counted to ten at least three times. Even so, his voice was still a growl when he said, "Where would you like to go?"

"Well, it was your invitation—at least it was sort of an invitation," she said. "So it's up to you. Since neither one of us is really dressed for it, we'd better rule out someplace fancy. Not that I mind being seen in jeans, but you have your reputation to consider."

If it hadn't been too late to get a reservation for "someplace fancy," Wolfe would have taken her to the best place in town *and* suffered the indignity of being given a tie by the maître d' just so he could have watched her regret her blithe words. She would have, surely. Even the most self-confident woman would have felt underdressed in jeans and a sweater.

He knew he was letting her get to him, he *knew* it. But he couldn't seem to help himself. Her light mockery grated on his nerves, and something else about her—he wasn't sure what—was affecting his senses in the most peculiar way. He couldn't decide if he wanted to strangle her, or to find out if her curiously erotic lips were as soft to the touch as they looked.

"I'm not hard to please," she was saying soulfully in that voice that was driving him crazy. "A crust of bread and a little water—"

Wolfe said something under his breath.

"Such language," she murmured.

He realized he hadn't even started the car. That he was sitting there, staring through the windshield and seeing absolutely nothing. That he was very tense, and didn't dare to look at her because he didn't know which impulse he'd obey if he did—choke her or kiss her. That he wanted a cigarette, and he'd never smoked in his life.

"For God's sake," he said, to himself but out loud.

She laughed suddenly. "Look, why don't we make this easier? Since I'm staying in a hotel, we can go to my suite and order room service. That way, as soon as you get fed up with me, you can walk out, and I'll already be home."

"I never walk out on dates."

"Really?" She sounded very polite. "Then maybe you are a gentleman born. I'll have to reserve judgment on that, though, because they *are* rare beasts."

Wolfe could feel himself tensing even more, despite every effort to relax taut muscles. Why couldn't he respond to her sarcasm with some of his own? Or, at the very least, shrug off the mockery without letting it affect him? He didn't know, but his growing tendency to take everything she said too seriously was yet another indication that she was having an unnervingly strong impact on him.

After a considerate pause to see if he had any response to make, Storm said, "If you're not crazy about being seen with me in a hotel—and who could blame you for that?—then we could always go to your place. Just stop someplace for hamburgers or a pizza—already cooked, of course."

"What—you mean you wouldn't cook for me?" he demanded sardonically, risking a glance at her. He looked so quickly that all he really saw was the flash of bright eyes and small white teeth as she grinned at him.

"Now, Wolfe," she said in a patient tone, "you *know* you don't want me to do that. Think of the precedent you'd be setting. It's a very dangerous one, you know. A man's taking his first steps down the road to domestication when he lets a woman cook for him. And a woman's got more than fun in mind when she goes to all that trouble."

He knew what she was saying. And, truth to tell, he'd always looked at it that way, whether it was true or not; he had made sure none of his women had ever cooked for him. But his curiosity, which had more than once led him into trouble, got the better of him. "Can you cook?" he asked her.

"Of course I can." She leaned toward him just a little and added in a conspiratorial tone, "In fact, I can actually cook with a real stove—no microwave required."

"Is there anything you can't do?"

"Along the lines of womanly little talents, you mean? Right offhand, I can't think of anything. I was raised by a very old-fashioned mama who truly believed there was such a thing as woman's work."

Starting the car at last, Wolfe said dryly, "So what happened to you?"

Unoffended, she laughed. "My daddy was a different sort, for which I am most grateful. What with him saying I had a good mind and had to study hard, and Mama teaching me how to make biscuits from scratch, I ended up with a goodly number of diverse talents."

Some part of Wolfe's mind had finally acknowledged the fact that her voice definitely was a part of the attraction he felt for her. And not just because it was a musical drawl that was oddly pleasing to the ear. Like most people who had never been near the Southern states, his ideas of "the South" were culled from books and movies— and she sounded so damn Southern that it was like listening to someone from an entirely different world.

Completely against his will—and unconsciously— he was drawn into that world. His irritation with her faded, so that fascination took a stronger and stronger hold on him. He kept asking questions, prompting her to talk about her background, and her lazy answers led him to more questions. By the time he turned the car into the parking lot of a good—just not fancy—Italian restaurant half an hour or so later, he had more or less forgotten the friction between them.

"How many brothers?" he demanded as he parked the car.

"Six." She chuckled. "So I guess it's no wonder Mama sort of went overboard when she finally got a girl."

"Then they're all older than you?"

"Yeah. Bigger too. I mean, really bigger. They all took after Daddy, and I took after Mama."

"Do they all live in Louisiana?" he asked, since she'd told him that was where she'd grown up.

"No, we're pretty scattered. Three of my brothers are career military and the other three like to travel, so we're lucky if we can all be home for Christmas." She glanced around, realizing that they'd stopped. "Oh, are we here?"

"Hope you like Italian," he said.

"Very much."

Wolfe had parked the car and automatically got out to go around and open her door. She got out, this time without a comment on his manners, and turned to set Bear in the passenger seat. The little cat looked up at them rather dolefully, but didn't attempt to escape the car.

"I hope you're going to lock it up," Storm said to Wolfe as she made way for him to shut the door. "Bear wouldn't appreciate it if he got stolen."

"Any thief is more likely to be after my car than your cat," Wolfe retorted, "so he shouldn't take it personally." But he used the little electronic gadget on his key ring to lock the car. "Will he be all right in there?"

"He'll be fine. Cats are pretty solitary creatures, really, and Bear never minds being alone. Of course, I'd never shut him up in a car if it was too hot or cold, or for more than an hour or two at a time."

Wolfe hesitated, then said, "And what if he has to . . ."

"He went before we left the museum." Storm smiled up at him. "Since he spends his days with me, I always make provisions for his needs. Don't worry—he won't have an accident."

It struck Wolfe that talking to a woman about her cat's personal habits was not exactly what he was accustomed to, but her smile—surprisingly sweet and warm when it wasn't mocking—made the matter seem unimportant. And *that* was a fine way to be thinking, he criticized himself as they went into the restaurant. First her voice had gotten to him in some way he couldn't even define, and now her smile.

At some point—he wasn't sure when or where it had happened—he'd lost control of this situation.

That thought kept him silently occupied for the next few minutes. Storm excused herself as soon as they were shown to their table, saying that Bear was shedding and she needed to wash her hands. Despite the busy restaurant Wolfe felt peculiarly alone while she was gone, which told him even more about her impact on him.

He was so conscious of her when they were together that he felt her absence just as acutely as he felt her presence. That bothered him a lot. Even if his strongest emotion had so far been sheer irritation, he still didn't like it. Storm made him think of the catalysts he could remember studying in science class, a substance that forced a reaction simply by being there.

He ordered wine for them both, and drank half a glass while he was trying to reassure himself that Storm Tremaine was not going to become a complication in his life.

"You're frowning," she said, slipping into her chair before he'd realized she had returned.

He looked across the table at her, bothered by her and by a vague feeling that she had kept him deliberately off balance ever since they had first spoken this afternoon. He hadn't *lost* control, she had stolen it from him; that was what his instincts were trying to tell him. Part of him wanted to believe it. But those eyes of hers, such an unusual and vivid green, brilliant and fierce and alive, were also clear and honest. Surely there was nothing deceptive about her?

"You're imagining things," he told her.

"I'm a logical woman, remember? I don't *imagine* things that aren't there." Before he could respond to that, she was going on in the same lazy voice. "I ran into one of your Barbie dolls in the ladies' room."

"What?" It was the last thing he'd expected, and took his mind off whether she was being honest with him.

Still smiling, she turned her head a bit and nodded across the room. "That one, at the cozy little table by the window. She was very friendly. She told me—without any prompting from me, you understand—that you liked your Scotch with ice and your women wearing nothing at all."

Wolfe turned his head cautiously and immediately spotted Nyssa Armstrong, a tall, blond woman of about thirty-five who was beautiful, sophisticated—and very much his type. She was with a bored-looking dark man who didn't appear interested even when Nyssa smiled across the room at Wolfe and wiggled her fingers at him.

He nodded to her, then looked back at Storm. She seemed highly amused. He cleared his throat. "Nyssa isn't a Barbie doll; trust me on that. She's smart."

"She's also very interested in *Mysteries Past*," Storm said. "And she knew who I was. Did you tell her I was the new computer technician?"

Wolfe could feel a frown drawing his brows together. "No. I haven't talked to her in days."

"Interesting, huh? It's also interesting to find her here." Storm sipped her wine and then shrugged. "Maybe a coincidence, but not a real likely one. Don't you think? I mean, this is a nice place and all, but I wouldn't guess it was her usual kind of haunt."

He knew he was still frowning, but Wolfe didn't comment on her observation. Instead he picked up his menu and said, "Why don't we order?"

Storm didn't object, and she gave her order to the

waitress a few minutes later. But it was obvious she had no intention of dropping the subject of Nyssa's presence, because as soon as the waitress collected their menus and went away, she said, "A party up on Nob Hill seems more like her usual habitat, I'd say. Am I right about that?"

"That's where she lives," Wolfe admitted, picking up a breadstick and snapping it neatly in half.

There was a slight pause, and then Storm said dryly, "At the moment I'm less concerned about her interest in you than her interest in the exhibit."

Wolfe looked up quickly. "So am I."

Storm chuckled, a warm, rich sound. "Okay, then stop resisting the subject. Since you and I are both involved in the security for the exhibit, and since I can adapt a computer program to guard against threats—if I know about them—maybe you'd better tell me the lady's story."

"I didn't say she was a threat," Wolfe protested.

One of Storm's delicate blond eyebrows rose in an expression of mockery. "Let me guess. Chivalry? Once you sleep with a lady you never utter a word to mar her good name?"

He could feel the ache in his jaw that told him his teeth were gritted. It was becoming a familiar sensation. "I knew it was too good to last. You couldn't force yourself to go an hour without getting scornful about something, could you?"

The eyebrow stayed up, and her lips curved to show even more of a taunt. "Certainly not—it's too much fun. You rise to the bait so wonderfully."

"Hasn't anyone warned you about fishing in dangerous waters? You're liable to catch something you can't handle."

"Promises, promises," she murmured, then laughed when his frown deepened. "Oh, stop scowling, Wolfe. I won't ask personal questions about—what was her name? Nyssa? That figures. Anyway, I won't ruffle your fur by asking questions about the private relationship between you two. It's none of my business, at least not at the moment."

He eyed her. "Not at the moment?"

"You never know when something like that could change." Before he could respond to her gentle statement, she went on briskly, "All I want to know is whatever you can tell me about her interest in the Bannister collection, which you and I are both responsible for protecting."

Wolfe hesitated, but it was a legitimate subject for her to raise—especially if Nyssa had made a point of introducing herself in the ladies' room, and if she did indeed know that Storm was the computer technician at the museum.

"She knew who you were? No kidding?" he asked.

"No kidding. And she didn't just know that I was installing the computer security system—she knew my name. That's the part that set off bells. How could she know my name, Wolfe? You didn't. Nobody at the museum did. And even my boss at Ace wasn't sure I'd be able to take the job until yesterday. I packed in a hurry and came over from Paris on the Concorde, so it's not like there was a lot of time for anyone to find out very much about me. So how did she?"

Wolfe sent a quick glance across the room, finding Nyssa and her companion eating their meal and apparently having a casual discussion. "I don't know." He looked back at Storm, a bit unsettled to realize that her brilliant eyes were graver than he'd yet seen them.

Storm shrugged a little, her gaze still locked with his. "Since I like to know what my security programs are supposed to be protecting, my boss filled me in. I had already heard about the Bannister collection. I've even seen all the pictures from the last time it was exhibited. What was that—more than thirty years ago?"

"About that," Wolfe agreed. "Lloyd's of London insures the collection, which is why I'm here."

She nodded. "So I was told; you're their top security expert. That's one reason Max Bannister asked for you. Another reason, I imagine, is because he knew very well he could trust you—since you're his half brother."

It was Wolfe's turn to nod. He wasn't very surprised that she knew about the relationship; he knew she'd talked to Morgan, and Morgan was aware that he and Max were half brothers. He didn't speak immediately, leaning back to allow the waitress to place his plate on the table. When she had served Storm and gone, he said, "That's right. Is it important?"

"That you're his brother?" Storm shrugged again, beginning to eat almost absentmindedly. "Probably not, but it never hurts to know these things. Is Nyssa aware of the relationship?"

He hesitated. "I don't think so. She's never mentioned it, at any rate."

Thoughtfully Storm said, "It isn't something that's generally known, so maybe not. Unless she found out from him. They move in the same circles, I'd guess."

"And you'd be right." Wolfe was watching her very intently even as he began eating his own meal. He was seeing yet another aspect of her personality, and it definitely intrigued him. Judging by the way she was talking, she seemed to have a puzzle-oriented mind much like his own, which was a surprise. Then again, since she was a crackerjack computer programmer, perhaps it shouldn't have surprised him.

"I don't suppose you'd want to disturb him on his honeymoon?" she ventured.

"Not if I have a choice," Wolfe replied dryly. "Why? To ask about Nyssa?"

Storm picked up a breadstick and nibbled on it for a moment, the look in her eyes abstracted, then shrugged. "I guess it really doesn't matter whether she realizes you two are brothers. I don't see how she could use the knowledge. She knows you're in charge of security for the exhibit, she knows what I'm responsible for, and she knows Max. As far as I can tell, she's been pretty blunt about her interest to all of us. True?"

"She's tried for years to persuade Max to let her see the collection," Wolfe said.

Storm waited a moment, then smiled. "And what did she try to persuade you to do?"

The dry tone made Wolfe feel uncomfortable, even though he'd been perfectly aware of Nyssa's aim from the first time they had danced together. Evenly he replied, "To see the collection before the exhibit opened to the public."

"I gather you resisted her blandishments," Storm said in a solemn voice.

"That better not be a question," he said.

Her unexpectedly sweet smile lit up her face. "Perish the thought. Would I cast aspersions on your honesty?"

"Probably."

She chuckled. "Well, I won't." She ate for a few moments in silence, then went on with the original subject. "Since your lady friend has been so open about her wishes, I can't see her as a threat to the security of the collection."

"Neither can I."

"But I still want to know how she found out about me. Granted, I wasn't exactly a secret, but she shouldn't have been able to find out my name."

Wolfe agreed with that. The problem was, he could think of only one way she might have gained the knowledge. Despite Max's faith in the company, Ace Security already had two strikes against them. One of their employees had, admittedly under pressure of blackmail, given valuable information to a thief, the result of which had been an attempt to rob the museum. And their previous computer technician had done a dandy job of wrecking weeks of work, even if it had been accidental.

What if there was a third strike against Ace? What if Nyssa had bribed or otherwise persuaded someone inside the company to provide her with information? And if so, what was she really up to? Was her stated desire the true one, that she simply wanted to see the Bannister collection before any other collectors were allowed a glimpse?

Or was she a genuine threat to the collection?

Storm seemed to be following his thoughts with uncanny accuracy. "Does she know anything about computers?" she asked, a glance across the room making it obvious that she was referring to Nyssa.

Wolfe shook his head slightly. "I don't know for sure, but I'd have to guess yes. She's known to have an outstanding business mind, so it's likely she has experience with computers." He looked across the table to find Storm watching him with something in her eyes he hadn't seen before. There was a shadow there, he thought. A secret.

"Want to set a trap?" she asked casually.

"Why would I want to do that? Risking the collection would be stupid—and definitely not my job," he said.

Storm smiled slightly. "No, but it's always better to take a risk when you can have more control. According to what I read in today's newspapers, this city seems to be crawling with thieves right now. There's a gang nobody can get near, the usual assorted independent thieves who always threaten valuables—and Quinn. Chances are, some or all of them will consider the *Mysteries Past* exhibit a very nice target."

"Undoubtedly," Wolfe said.

"Then why wait for them to come knocking at your door? Why not open the door just a little and see who can't resist the temptation to come in."

He pushed his plate away and picked up his wineglass, giving himself a moment. "What kind of trap do you have in mind?" he asked finally.

"Well, let's look at what we have. After the change-over the museum's security will be state-of-the-art electronics. Now, since there's an independent power supply that isn't accessible from the outside of the building, a thief's best bet would be to control the system with another computer."

Immediately Wolfe said, "Our system's completely enclosed. There's no modem, and no tie-in to the phone lines. So how could anyone outside gain access?"

Storm hesitated, her eyes oddly still. Then she pushed her own plate away and leaned back. "You remember this afternoon, when I was under the desk straightening out cables?"

"Yeah."

"Well, I found something else under there. Somebody had patched in a pretty handy connection to an old, unused phone line in that room. So I'd say that at least one thief has already unlocked the door to the system."

By the time they reached Storm's hotel suite nearly an hour later, Wolfe had stopped swearing out loud. But he paced like his namesake caged, barely noticing the room he was in.

Storm bent to allow her cat to transfer from her shoulder to the back of the couch, where he made himself comfortable. Then she sat down at one end. Both she and Bear watched the man moving around the room.

"It had to be the first technician," he said finally.

"It wasn't him."

He stopped pacing to stare at her. "If you're trying to be loyal to Ace—"

"I'm not," she interrupted. "Look, Wolfe, if I or any other decent technician wanted to patch into a phone line, we could do it without leaving a lot of evidence. What I saw looked like it had been done in one hell of a hurry. Anybody could have gotten into that room at some point during the past weeks, you know that. The hallway isn't guarded, not now when the security system isn't on-line. And I'm willing to bet my predecessor didn't spend every minute in there, especially when the machine was loading information and he didn't have anything to do except wait for it to finish."

Wolfe had to admit, if only silently, that he hadn't thought much about the security of the computer room himself. It was as she said—though the machines themselves were certainly valuable, nobody could cart them from the museum unobserved, and the system wasn't vitally important until it was on-line, so that hallway had not been the focus of the guards' attention.

"Dammit," he muttered.

Storm shrugged. "Hey, they've got an unlocked door, not an open one. I can lock it for good by cutting the connection. Or I can stand ready at the door and see who tries to open it."

"We're back to the trap," he said, crossing the room to sit down on the arm of the couch across from her.

"Well, it makes sense to me." Storm wrestled her boots off and then curled up at her end of the couch. "Since the original security program turned out to be too accessible to a thief—my boss told me about that, by the way—I was brought in to install a program so new it isn't in anybody's computer. Except this one." She tapped her temple with one finger.

Wolfe nodded. "That's what Max and I agreed to,

providing we see the entire program before it goes on-line."

"Which you will. But the point is that even if somebody has an unlocked door into the system, getting in won't be easy at all. They'll have to figure out what the access codes are, and I designed tough ones."

"But they could still get in?"

"Oh, sure. Given enough time, patience, and knowledge. They'll have to make a number of attempts, however. So all I have to do is program the system to guard itself. If there's an attempted entry, I'll be alerted."

"Could we find out who was trying to get in?"

"Maybe. We could try tracing the phone line."

"You don't sound too hopeful," Wolfe noted.

She smiled wryly. "If it was me trying to get in, I would have routed the call through so many lines you'd never find me. Any competent technician would do the same."

After brooding for a few moments in silence, Wolfe said, "Then your idea of a trap isn't to catch somebody in the system, it's to lead them to a place where we're waiting for them."

Her smile was quick and approving. "Exactly. If I know they're trying to get into the system, I can have a little subprogram all ready to tell them whatever we want them to know. Like the system has a weak spot that looks just too inviting for words? No thief worth his—or her—salt is going to pass that up."

What she was saying was reasonable, but Wolfe wasn't quite ready to approve her idea. First, if a thief was after the Bannister collection, he—or she—wouldn't make a move until the collection was in the museum. And second, he wasn't sure that he completely trusted Storm Tremaine. That shadowy, secret expression in her eyes earlier had bothered him.

So he said, "I'll have to think about it. In the morning I'll want you to show me that phone patch."

"Of course," she murmured. "After all, I might have some nefarious plan of my own. So you'd better give the matter all due consideration."

Either his mistrust had shown more plainly than he'd thought or else she was developing a unique talent for reading his expression; whichever it was, he didn't like it.

"I didn't mean—" he began.

"Oh, don't bother to deny it, Wolfe. I can certainly understand your position. I mean, the exhibit isn't even in place yet, and there have already been so many problems. And I'm sure you'd feel just awful if somebody you were seeing personally—like Nyssa, say—actually turned out to be a thief bent on stealing your brother's priceless collection."

He could feel himself tensing yet again. That drawling voice, dammit. And she had a knack for putting things in such a way that they really did sound insulting.

"I am not seeing her," he said through gritted teeth. "Not now, anyway."

Storm's expressive face took on a look of spurious sympathy. "Yeah, she was another who didn't last long, wasn't she? Have you considered therapy?"

"There's nothing wrong with me!" he practically roared.

She blinked. "No, of course not. Lots of men have a difficult time finding the right woman. But I still say you should broaden your horizons. I mean, you've got to be—what? Pushing forty?"

"Thirty-six," he snapped, telling himself to calm down because he was positive she was laughing at him.

"Oh, sorry—thirty-six," she said solemnly. "Well, still. You must have been concentrating on your favorite kind of blonde for twenty years now. I'd think that by this time common sense would have told you that whatever it is you're looking for, it isn't there."

Wolfe knew he was being deliberately maneuvered. Ever since their first conversation this afternoon, she had been doing it to him, and knowing she was didn't seem to make much difference. He was even sure that if he stopped and thought about it, he'd come to the conclusion that she had brought up his social preferences every time he had ventured into some area she didn't want to talk about.

The problem was, that drawling voice of hers was making him crazy, and the gleam in her eyes—be it laughter or the sheer brilliance of her intelligence—affected his emotions rather than his mind. It was very difficult for him to think about anything except that she was making him crazy.

And since she'd kept him off balance for much of the past hours, it wasn't really surprising that he reacted to her now out of instinct and emotion.

"What makes you so damn sure *you've* got what I'm looking for?" he demanded, leaving the arm of the couch to move closer to her. Since she was sitting sideways on the couch with her feet up, his thigh pressed against her hip.

"I didn't say that," she murmured, her ridiculously long lashes dropping to veil the brilliant eyes.

"The hell you didn't. You've been saying it all day. What's wrong, Storm? Didn't you think I'd get curious?"

Her dark lashes rose as she looked at him, and her eyes were quite definitely laughing. Gravely she said, "Now, don't do anything you'll regret later. We both know I've goaded you into this, and if you let me get away with it . . . I'll always know which buttons to push. Won't I?"

That was true, and he realized it. But there was something utterly disarming about her wry acknowledgment of her own provocative behavior.

And besides that, he had felt tantalized by her all evening, attracted and irritated, amused and angered, fascinated and defensive; even with all his inner alarms jangling a warning, he simply couldn't be sensible about her.

For the second time that day he said, "I know I'm going to regret this." Then he pulled her into his arms.

What he felt in those first few moments was not regret. She was warm in his arms, slender and almost frighteningly delicate. Her mouth was as soft beneath his as he'd thought it would be, and her upper body molded itself to his instantly.

He hadn't expected what happened then. It was like a detonation, an explosion of sensation so intense that it jarred his entire body and shocked his mind. His instinct was to draw back, to shy away from something so extreme, but when he did so, her eyes opened and caught him.

They were dark green, glowing with heat now instead of light, and they were shocked. Her lips were parted, trembling, and she seemed to him a little pale. Then the shock faded, replaced by a sweet, shy eagerness, and her arms lifted slowly to slide around his neck.

Wolfe muttered a curse, but his head bent to hers again. Now her erotic mouth was alive under his, and there was so much heat between them that he knew they were both going to get burned. He could feel her surprisingly full breasts pressed to his chest, and his fingers were tangled in her glorious hair, and she made a husky little sound that went to his head like raw brandy.

For one eternal instant he almost gave in and let the passion carry them both away, but the alarm bells were going off wildly inside him and he couldn't ignore them any longer.

Storm wasn't immediately aware that he was going to leave her, and when she did realize, it took her a moment or so to find her voice. "Did I do something wrong?" she murmured, feeling too dazed to consider the question.

His face was very hard, but his eyes were burning like the blue of a flame. "Yeah," he answered, his voice both soft and curiously harsh. "You met me."

Before she could even begin to figure that out, the door closed quietly behind him.

She turned slowly, lowering her feet to the floor, and sat there gazing across the room at nothing. It had been a very long day. She hadn't yet been in San Francisco twenty-four hours, and already she was in trouble.

"Yah," Bear said, as if he'd read her mind.

"I can handle it," she said, turning her head to look at the little cat. He was sitting on the back of the couch, where he had observed silently. "I won't lose control. It's just jet lag, that's all. That's why I'm imagining things tonight."

Bear chirped softly.

She didn't want to admit to herself that weariness had never made her imagine things before, especially a desire so powerful it had hit her with the numbing force of a blow. She didn't want to admit she'd never in her life felt anything like that.

But it was true nonetheless.

As tired and disturbed as she was, Storm's inner alarm clock reminded her of an appointment that had to be kept. She rose and went into the bathroom and splashed cold water on her face, pausing for a moment to study her reflection in the mirror. Her lips were a little swollen, a deeper red than she was accustomed to, and her eyes were very bright, almost feverish.

"Liar," she murmured to herself, admitting what was gnawing at her painfully. "And the hell of it is— you're getting good at it."

She dried her face and went back out into the

sitting room, trying not to think. Not that she could avoid it. The intensity of desire between her and Wolfe had caught her off guard, the passion it promised a definite complication. It wasn't her job to get involved with a man—and most especially not the man responsible for the security of the *Mysteries Past* exhibit.

She couldn't afford to let that happen, she told herself fiercely. Even if it caused no other problems, her loyalty could be divided. She could let down her guard with Wolfe, tell him things she had no right to tell him.

Even worse, she would be gaining his trust under false pretenses. He was, like his namesake, wary, suspicious of a hand held out; what would his reaction be if they became lovers and he found out she'd lied to him?

"Damn," she whispered, unconsciously pacing the sitting room as Bear watched silently from the back of the couch.

A soft knock at the door drew Storm's attention, and she went quickly to the little hallway. She looked through the security peephole and immediately opened the door. Without a word she stepped back to let him in.

While she was closing the door he went into the sitting room, automatically looking around him with the searching gaze of a man always wary of his surroundings. Bear spoke to him softly from the back of the couch, and he scratched the little cat briefly under the chin as he passed. He ended up standing to one side of the window, gazing out on the lights of the city.

Storm came back into the room and sat down on the arm of a chair, watching him. "I don't like lying to him."

The man turned away from the window, his strange eyes cool and calm. "You don't have a choice," he said.

Three

Storm smothered a yawn with one hand while she used the other to key a brief command into the computer. It began humming busily, obedient to her touch.

"Yarr," Bear commented from his position atop the desk.

"Not so loud." Storm lifted her coffee mug and sipped the steaming liquid cautiously. It was her third cup since arriving at the museum at eight-thirty, and the caffeine was only now kicking in an hour later. Normally she limited herself to one cup, since caffeine had the peculiar effect of making her more reckless than usual, but she told herself that this one time it was more important to wake up and function with something approaching a normal efficiency than to worry about being reckless.

A night's sleep had done little to combat her jet lag, and she felt as though she were moving through a fog. In addition, she hated mornings just on principle, so her mood wouldn't have been much improved even if she'd been at the top of her form.

She hoped Wolfe wouldn't come into the computer room anytime soon. She hadn't yet seen him this morning, and that was fine with her. If he discovered just how punchy she was first thing in the morning, he was certainly both intelligent enough and ruthless enough to take advantage of it.

An image of waking up in bed beside him rose in her mind, and she hastily pushed it away, feeling heat in her face. God, the man had really gotten to her—and that was so unusual it disturbed her deeply.

She had dreamed about him last night, first an incredibly erotic interlude between them as lovers and then, in one of those crazy, topsy-turvy changes common to dreams, the scene had turned into something else. She'd been in a peculiar kind of classroom feverishly writing mathematical formulas on a blackboard draped with glittering gems while telling herself out loud, over and over, that she had to do her job. Then another change of scene and she was running, hiding, while Wolfe, enraged, hunted her through a creepy jungle filled with computer cables instead of vines; he kept yelling that she'd betrayed him.

Storm had awakened just as Wolfe, turning into his namesake, had lunged at her in the dream. She hadn't, as with most nightmares, awakened in gasping, heart-thudding fear. What she had felt had been an anguish so acute it had stabbed at her, and there had been tears on her face.

For a moment as she sat there at her quiet desk remembering the details of the dream, Storm was tempted just to run. But even as the urge occurred her mind was listing all the reasons why she couldn't.

Having a logical intellect and a strong sense of responsibility definitely had its drawbacks.

Sighing, Storm double-checked the computer to make certain it was loading properly, and then reached for the thick cardboard tube leaning against her desk. From this she withdrew a set of blueprints for the museum, which she spread out atop her desk.

The edges kept trying to roll up, so she used an amiable Bear to weight one corner, a thick manual on the workings of the laser security system to weight another, then her telephone and coffee mug on the remaining two corners.

It helped to have something her mind could focus on, and since she had rashly promised Wolfe she would have the computerized security system online in record time, she had her work cut out for her. After studying the first-floor plans for some time, she got a legal pad from her desk drawer and a handful of sharpened pencils from another. Her favorite bright pink highlighter pen was in the breast pocket of her flannel shirt, and she used that to mark specific points directly on the blueprints.

She left the computer room only once in the next hour, going across the hall to the employees' lounge to refill her coffee cup. She met no one on the way, and didn't linger.

It was nearly eleven o'clock when a brisk rap on the jamb of the open door heralded Morgan West's entrance into the room. The young director of the *Mysteries Past* exhibit looked as elegant as usual, her gleaming black hair worn up today and her astonishing figure simply clothed in a jade silk blouse and black pants.

Storm, dressed in faded jeans and a green plaid flannel shirt worn open over a black turtleneck sweater, felt a pang of rueful envy for the other woman's effortless sense of elegance.

"Hi," Morgan said as she breezed in.

"Hi, yourself," Storm responded. "What's up?"

Amber eyes bright with interest, Morgan rested a hip on one corner of the desk, automatically scratched Bear under the chin, and said mildly, "Wolfe's acting like he got one paw caught in a steel trap."

Storm frowned down at her most recent note and began to erase one word. "Yeah?"

"Yeah. And since one of the guards saw you two

leave together last night, the place is filled with speculation."

Storm had thought it might be. She gave up the pretense of working and leaned back in her chair. "So you're in charge of officially verifying the facts?" she asked politely.

Morgan chuckled warmly. "Not at all. I'm just incurably nosy. I'm also very impressed—if, that is, you *are* responsible for Wolfe's lousy mood."

"Oh? Why is that?"

"Because, from what I've seen these last months, Wolfe hasn't let any lady get close enough to even barely annoy him, much less get under his skin to the point that he's snapping everybody's head off."

"As I understand it," Storm commented dryly, "he's let plenty of ladies get close."

"Oh, physically, sure. But not emotionally. Even Nyssa Armstrong couldn't make a dent, and she's been enslaving men since she hit her teens."

Storm pursed her lips thoughtfully. "I somehow doubt Wolfe could be enslaved by any woman." She kept to herself the thought that it was likely to be the other way around.

Morgan half nodded in agreement. "He'd have to be willing, that's for sure. The right woman could do it. Is that you, by any chance?"

"I'm not his type," Storm replied placidly.

It was obvious by then that Morgan wasn't going to get the answers she'd been probing for, and her chuckle this time held graceful acceptance. "Okay, okay, I know when I'm being warned off. But just for the record, I think the reason Wolfe's snapping at everybody is because you *are* his type—and he's getting real nervous about it."

Storm smiled slightly, but all she said was, "I'll note down your opinion. For the record."

Morgan's smile grew wider. "You know, both you and Wolfe are so closemouthed you'll drive each other nuts. Oh, boy, is this going to be good. I'll get myself a front-row seat and just watch from the sidelines, shall I?"

"Suit yourself."

Laughing, Morgan removed herself from the desk. "Listen, if you don't get a better offer, I know a great café just around the corner where we could have lunch. Interested?"

"Sure," Storm said, adding blandly, "If I don't get a better offer."

"Well, give me a call if you do. I'll be in my office the rest of the morning."

"Gotcha."

For a few minutes after Morgan had gone, Storm remained at her desk, looking blindly down at the blueprints. Morgan, she thought, would make a first-class friend. She was talkative, yes, but honest and without an ounce of malice. But she was also unusually perceptive, highly observant, and very, very smart—and that was why Storm couldn't drop her guard with the other woman. Not now, at least. And depending on how things turned out, maybe not ever.

That thought was a reminder of her responsibilities, and a glance at her watch confirmed the time. Storm rose from the desk and went to shut the door firmly. She had already discovered that this room, like most meant to house sensitive electronic equipment, was specially insulated and virtually soundproofed, so she had no qualms about using the phone. Especially since she had done some quick rewiring yesterday and used a couple of state-of-the-art devices to ensure that no one could pick up another phone in the building and eavesdrop on the line she was using.

She made herself comfortable in her chair, mentally organized her thoughts, and picked up the receiver. She punched a number from memory,

48 • KAY HOOPER

and her call was answered on the first ring.

"Yeah?"

"It's me. I've spent the morning going over the blueprints. For a big building with too many doors, this place is pretty tight."

"Can you handle the security system?" he asked.

"Of course I can. I already told you that."

"All right, don't get your Irish up; I had to ask."

"Ireland was a few generations back," she said dryly. "And only on one side. These days my temper's pure Cajun."

He sighed, about halfway amused. "I'll keep that in mind." Then his rather cool voice turned businesslike again. Businesslike and definitely critical. "I'm not so sure you should have told Wolfe about the phone patch. Not this early, anyway. He was already suspicious of Ace Security; this is not going to help."

Storm kept her voice calm. "I believe I was able to use something else to deflect his suspicions away from security precautions."

"What did you use?"

"I pointed him at Nyssa Armstrong."

There was a long silence, and then his voice came over the line very softly. "You did what?"

"You heard me."

"Why the hell didn't you tell me this last night?"

Gently she said, "Because I didn't see the need to. And since I'm the one in the hot seat, it's my call."

Another long silence, and when he spoke, it was obvious he was holding on to a formidable temper. "I see. Then do you mind telling me—"

A firm knock on the door, loud enough for him to hear, interrupted him. Quickly he said, "Call me again later."

"Wait," she said. Raising her voice, she invited the visitor to enter. Since the knock had been so emphatic, she wasn't at all surprised when Wolfe came in. "Be with you in a minute," she told him calmly, and then, into the phone, said, "You were saying?"

"It's him, isn't it? He's right there in the room?"

"Yes." She watched Wolfe close the door behind him.

The silence this time was brief, and the voice on the phone was unwillingly amused. "You'd play with dynamite in a forest fire, wouldn't you, Storm?"

"Sure. It's in my résumé."

He sighed. "Well, never mind. Just call me when you're free and we'll set up the next meeting. We have to discuss this before it goes all to hell."

"I'll do that. Thank you very much, sir."

He made a rude noise—obviously because he knew her courtesy was for Wolfe's benefit—and hung up.

Storm cradled the phone and looked at the visitor towering over her desk. Judging by his impassive face, he wasn't going to mention last night. In a voice dripping with politeness she drawled, "Is there something I can do for you?"

Instead of answering, Wolfe said, "You mentioned your résumé. Planning to change jobs?"

"It's crossed my mind once or twice. Besides, it never hurts to keep your options open."

"I suppose." He looked as if he could have said more on the subject, but it was clear he wasn't suspicious of the call.

Before he could tell her why he'd come in, Storm, characteristically, strolled in where angels would have been hesitant to go. "I hear you've been a mite testy this morning," she offered solemnly.

His impassive mask cracked a bit as his mouth tightened. "Morgan talks too much."

Storm chuckled. "I doubt even Morgan would argue with that assessment. Comfort yourself with the knowledge that she has your best interests at heart."

"I don't need her help," Wolfe snapped. "And I want her to mind her own business."

Storm leaned an elbow on the blueprints, propped her chin in her hand, and gently drawled, "People in hell want ice water; that don't mean they get it."

Wolfe stared at her. For the life of him, he couldn't think of a thing to say.

She smiled slightly. "Something my mama used to tell her kids. In other words, what you want doesn't count for a whole lot. You won't shut Morgan up without a gag, and even if you did, someone else would be happy to spread the news that you were something less than your usual calm self."

He couldn't deny the truth of that. And even more, he knew he was only making matters worse by his attitude now. It wasn't as if he was hiding anything. He was in a rotten mood, and everyone knew it.

Part of him wanted to hang on to that mood, because it provided a sort of insulation between his turbulent feelings and the cause of all that chaos—her. If he stayed mad, he wouldn't let himself think about how she looked and sounded and about how much he wanted to touch her. But, as usual, her lazy voice and vivid face had the trick of both fascinating and irritating him until he found himself answering her taunts and jabs instead of letting them roll off his back.

Like now, for instance.

"Little bit under the weather, Wolfe? Get up on the wrong side of the bed? Or maybe you just had a hard time sleeping last night?"

"None of the above," he retorted. "And if that last was a passing reference to the haunting effect of your charms—"

"It was."

Distracted, he said severely, "Don't you have an ounce of feminine guile?"

"Not even a spoonful," Storm said with a faintly wistful expression that was disarming.

He tried not to let himself be disarmed. "Well, cultivate it, why don't you? It's not exactly subtle to ask a man if you gave him a sleepless night."

"Maybe not, but I'm curious. Did I?"

Somewhat grimly Wolfe said, "I wouldn't answer that if it was my ticket into heaven."

Storm smiled at him. "You just did. Why, Wolfe, I had no idea my—charms, didn't you say?—were so potent."

He drew a deep breath and tried to hold on to his temper, his resolve, and his wits—in pretty much that order. "Look, I didn't come in here to discuss anything except business."

"Chicken," she murmured.

Wolfe gritted his teeth. He was *not* going to let her get to him again. No way. He was completely in control. "I came in to take a look at that phone patch."

Storm didn't immediately respond since the computer's beep announced the need for a new floppy disk. She got the machine busily working again, then returned her gaze to Wolfe. Between his refusal to admit anything unusual had happened between them and the fact that she'd had way too much coffee, it probably shouldn't have surprised Storm to feel a rush of dangerous recklessness. In fact, it didn't surprise her, because she was completely caught up in the impulse.

She didn't get up from her chair. Instead she pushed it back a foot or so and slightly to one side, leaving barely enough room for Wolfe to get underneath the desk. She produced a flashlight from a bottom drawer of the desk, set it on top, and then sat back in her chair and said, "Be my guest."

If he hesitated, it was only for a second. He came around the desk, picked up the flashlight, and went down on one knee. "Where is it?" he asked somewhat tautly.

"Right side, toward the front of the desk," she answered. "Where the phone lines are run up through the floor."

He was so close she could feel the heat of his body, and memories of the night before rose up in her mind. How could he refuse to admit anything had happened between them? Just sitting here, with him so close, it seemed impossible for her to keep her hands to herself. She felt a wild urge to touch him, an almost overwhelming need to know he was as shaken by this as she was.

But perhaps he wasn't. She had to consider that, given his lifestyle. Even if he had suffered a sleepless night, it didn't have to mean anything except his resistance to getting involved with her. Perhaps Wolfe could detach himself completely, feeling desire only when he wanted to. She wasn't his type, after all. And she could have imagined—or at least exaggerated—the explosion of desire between them last night.

It was entirely possible, she thought painfully, that he felt nothing for her except a male's virtually automatic temptation for an attractive and available female.

The most painful thing of all to Storm was that that possibility didn't seem to matter. She couldn't even look away from him. Her fingers laced together tightly in her lap as she watched his head and shoulders disappear under the desk. Her gaze moved over the broad strength of his back, the sleek skin and rippling muscles she imagined covered now by a dark shirt and the black leather jacket he usually wore.

Storm wondered vaguely if that black leather meant what it had seemed to mean in her girlhood. It had been a symbol then, she remembered, a warning of danger. In the relatively small Southern town where she'd grown up, black leather was something reserved for the wildest of teenagers, boys and girls. It had stood for taking chances, for bucking authority, for being strong enough to stand alone and daring enough to flaunt it.

Her adult mind told her now that black leather was just another bit of fashion, a type of material used for jackets and coats and skirts—not a symbol of anything much. But she had a purely emotional feeling that on Wolfe, black leather still meant danger.

He came out from under the desk and sat back on his heels. Turning off the flashlight, he set it on the desk and said, "You were right; it does look like it was done in a hurry." He didn't meet her eyes.

They were so close to each other that Storm's knee was touching the black leather covering his arm. She didn't want to talk about phone patches, but heard her voice emerge huskily. "It wouldn't have taken long. Five, ten minutes if they knew what they were doing." Utterly fascinated, she watched a muscle bunch underneath the tan skin of his jaw.

Wolfe had known almost immediately after walking into her office a few minutes ago that he couldn't deny it any longer; he was hip-deep in trouble and sinking fast. Looking into her vivid face and hearing that indolent drawl was like being touched with an electric current; he felt more alive when he was near her than he had ever felt before. The difference was so striking it was as if he had been merely going through the motions until now, and feeling almost nothing.

What she made him feel could barely be contained. It had required all his will to stand across the desk from her and carry on a conversation—even one of their usual snappy ones—without completely giving himself away; when he had gone around the desk and knelt so close to her, his resolve to avoid getting involved with her began to splinter. And he had to ask himself why he was fighting so hard. Why was he so angry about this? An attraction so powerful had to be positive rather than negative.

Didn't it?

He hadn't been able to control his voice. He could smell her perfume, something curiously exotic that had followed him home last night and into his dreams. He had barely been able to examine the phone patch under the desk.

And when he backed out from under the desk, it became even harder to concentrate on business, until it became impossible. His last hope was to avoid looking into her vibrant green eyes, because he knew if he did, he'd be caught in them. And he had a strong feeling that once caught in that snare, he'd never again be able to call his soul his own. Or his heart.

He started to get up, but he turned toward her as he went onto one knee, until they were almost facing each other—and he froze when, without thinking, she reached out to him. Her fingertips touched his dark shirt. Silk, she realized, and a part of her found the contrast between black leather and dark silk oddly compelling. Dangerous, she thought, but elegant too.

His eyes finally met hers, and they were like the pure, searing blue at the base of a flame. She didn't even feel her fingers move to brush the collar of his shirt aside, and the sensation of hard, warm skin under her touch was such a shock that it caught at her breath and jerked her eyes away from his as she looked at her hand. She was touching him just below the base of his throat, and the open neck of his shirt invited her to go farther down where there was a hint of the thick auburn hair covering his chest.

When she lifted her gaze to meet his again, Storm could feel the breath catch in her throat, feel her heart skip a beat and then begin thudding in a heavy, quickening rhythm.

Wolfe turned slowly the rest of the way until they faced each other completely. His hands lifted to her denim-covered knees, the weight of them warm and hard. She didn't resist when he eased her legs apart, or when his hands slid up the outsides of her thighs to her hips and pulled her toward him.

He was on his knees before her, but he was no supplicant; the desire burning in his eyes was not a plea, it was a demand.

It was a starkly erotic position, and everything female in Storm responded wildly. Her inner thighs pressed against his sides just at his waist, and her hands lifted to his shoulders. They were almost eye to eye.

Huskily she said, "Did I give you a sleepless night, Wolfe?"

"Yes, dammit," he said, his voice as rough as the surface of granite but not hard at all. His hands were beneath her open flannel shirt, curving over her hips and then sliding up to span her tiny waist. He wanted to lift the hem of her black sweater and touch her skin, imagining the silky warmth of it, but he had a strong feeling that once he touched her like that he wouldn't be able to stop.

Her voice still husky, Storm said innocently, "But I'm not your type. How could I disturb your sleep?"

Wolfe pulled her even closer until she was on the very edge of her chair and he felt the firm mounds of her breasts touch his chest. He wanted to wrestle his leather jacket off and toss it aside because it was one of the barriers between them, but he couldn't take his hands off her long enough to do it.

"You're going to make me admit it, aren't you?" he muttered, his gaze fixed on the erotic softness of her lips. As he watched they curved in a little smile.

"I'm just asking a simple question."

"Then I'll answer it." His head bent toward her, his eyes still focused on her lips, and his voice roughened even more. "I'm taking your advice—broadening my horizons."

"It's about time," she whispered, just before his mouth covered hers.

Like the night before, Storm felt an instant burst of heat ignite somewhere deep inside her, so bright and hot she knew it was changing her just as surely as a crucible reshaped steel. She was being altered by Wolfe and his passion, by her own astonishing desire, transformed into a woman who understood something that had once been a mystery to her.

Now she knew how even a strong-willed and confident woman could be overwhelmed by her emotions and senses. How it was possible to reach out in wonder to the bright beauty of a flame even *knowing* it would burn painfully. Now she understood how there could be a hunger so acute it had to be satisfied no matter what the cost.

He was kissing her with the same intense hunger she felt herself, deep kisses that were starkly possessive, and her body responded beyond her control. Even through their clothing, she could feel the hardness of his chest against her aching breasts. Her position—with her legs practically wrapped around him—was so sexual it was as if they were already making love.

It was what Storm wanted, more than she had ever wanted anything in her life. She'd known this man barely twenty-four hours, but she felt no uncertainty on that point. Some things were beyond question, existing in fact, like the beat of her heart.

So her response to him was completely unrestrained. She met the intense desire of his kisses with her own fierce hunger, her arms tight around his neck, squirming to be even closer to him, her body out of her control. She had forgotten all about the unlocked door, and wouldn't have cared very much if someone had reminded her.

Wolfe had forgotten their lack of privacy himself. Her soft, enticing mouth was as feverish as his own, as hungry, her response to him so potent he had forgotten everything else, including his reservations and apprehensions about getting involved with her. Nothing seemed to matter except the feel of her slender body in his arms. The way she was moving against him sent his already burning desire soaring until he was on the verge of completely losing control.

He probably would have given up the struggle, but the clear tone of the computer's beep, so alien as it intruded on flesh-and-blood passions, recalled him partially to his senses. The machine was indicating its need for more information—and to Wolfe it was a glaring reminder of where they were.

He tore his mouth from hers, one of his hands lifting to cradle the back of her head and press her face against his neck. Her thick hair was as soft as silk, baby fine, and he fought the urge to bury his face in the luxuriant pale gold mass. "If I don't stop now..." he managed to warn her, his voice so harsh it sounded angry even to him.

Storm didn't seem to be the least bit afraid of him no matter how he sounded. She tried to burrow even closer, making a little sound of disappointment, and he could feel her warm lips moving against his skin. His entire body seemed to clench in an almost brutal jolt of raw need, and for an instant his arms tightened around her. If the computer hadn't beeped again just then, he probably would have given in to her and to his own need.

With an effort that nearly killed him, Wolfe put his hands on her shoulders and eased her back away from him. Trying to control his voice so it didn't sound rough, he said, "Storm, we can't. Not here."

She blinked at him. Her eyes were misty, like emeralds gleaming through fog, and her face was soft with yearning. He could feel her trembling.

"No," she said huskily, "I suppose not." Very slowly she drew her arms from around his neck, letting her hands drop to her thighs.

He couldn't let go of her, his fingers moving slightly to probe the delicate bones of her shoulders. Part of him insisted he simply stop this, back away and leave the room without another word, without getting in even deeper. But another part of him had already surrendered to desire, and it was that part he listened to.

"We can go somewhere," he said, making it a question, his voice low. "My place is closest."

Storm looked at him for a long moment in silence, her face still soft. But her eyes were clear now, as direct and honest as usual, and the faintly ironic drawl was back when she sighed and said, "You aren't going to like this, I'm afraid."

"I'm not going to like what?"

"What I have to say."

Wolfe released her shoulders and slowly sat back on his heels. A number of possibilities flitted through his mind, but what they all boiled down to was simple: She wasn't going with him back to his place. "And that is?"

Storm didn't flinch at the hardness of his voice, and she didn't look away from his suddenly stony face. "Despite what I said to you yesterday, I'm not really in the market for a husband right now. I could handle an affair. We both know I'm only going to be here a few weeks at most, then I'm gone to my next assignment—probably out of the country."

He nodded slightly, waiting.

She drew a quick breath, the only sign yet that this was more difficult for her than she was letting on. "What I can't handle, what I refuse to be, is a one-night stand—or even a three-day fling. I won't be a toy you play with for a while until you see the next one in a store window somewhere. I'm no Barbie doll, Wolfe."

"I know that," he said evenly.

"Do you?"

"Yes." He wanted to reach out for her again, but wouldn't let himself. "So what do you want from me? A promise?"

"No. I just have to know this means something to you, something other than having one more bedmate to add to the list. Once we settle that, I'll never bring up the subject again, no matter what happens between us. But I have to be sure of that much before this goes any further. I have to."

Looking into her grave eyes, he knew she wouldn't back down. The way she'd behaved from the beginning told him that. Storm Tremaine gave as good as she got—and quite often won the upper hand without apparent effort. Little she certainly was, but there was nothing small about her assurance or willpower. She wasn't intimidated by his superior strength, dismayed by his quick temper, or troubled by his own iron will.

And if she said there was one answer she needed from him before she was prepared to go any further, then that was precisely what she meant.

He also knew that if he hadn't stopped, she wouldn't have asked for that answer. If he had pulled her to the floor, or if he had made room for them on her desk and lifted her there, she would have given herself to him without hesitation. In his arms she was as blindly hungry as he was, and that knowledge—now—was maddening to him.

She wasn't asking for very much, but it was more than he was prepared to give. He wasn't ready to examine his own feelings about her, and he sure as hell wasn't ready to make any kind of a commitment. Even one lasting only a few weeks.

Wolfe got to his feet slowly and moved away from her, around the desk. He wished he could have said something flippant or careless, but that was beyond him. Instead, because he couldn't think of anything else, he simply ignored everything except business.

"I haven't made up my mind about using that tapped phone line as a trap. Am I wrong in assuming it doesn't become any kind of threat to the museum or the new exhibit until the program is completely written and loaded?"

"No, you aren't wrong." Her voice was as calm as his had been. "Anyone with enough expertise to tap into the line would know better than to try to find a hole in an incomplete security system. The holes don't become visible until the entire plan can be studied. There's really no possibility of a threat until the new system is complete and on-line."

"Then leave the patch in place and I'll let you know," he said. Without looking at her, he left the room.

He had closed the door behind him, and Storm gazed at it somewhat blindly as she sat back in her chair. She didn't want to think about much of anything, least of all why she had issued an ultimatum to Wolfe, but it was impossible not to. She had done it out of a sense of honesty, knowing herself too well not to believe that a brief fling with Wolfe would have been hideously destructive to her—and she would have struck out at him in her pain. So she asked for more than a fling.

That was simple enough, clear and the truth. What was more complicated, and less clear, was her other reason for trying to stop the headlong rush toward consummated passion. It had to do with honesty. Or, rather, the lack thereof. It had to do with duplicity.

She had also asked because she had known it was too soon, that he would draw away—perhaps for good. She had deliberately used his reluctance to stop something over which she seemed to have very little control. Because she wanted him so badly and didn't trust herself to keep her head about it, she had forced him to say no.

Not very honest, perhaps, but Storm was only trying—rather desperately—to avoid a much greater deceit. If they became lovers, the question of trust became increasingly important. Once they were intimate, it was likely Wolfe would trust her more and more. And that was what she was afraid of. As long as he was even mildly suspicious of her, or at least a bit wary, she couldn't really hurt him with her lies.

But what would happen if they were lovers when he discovered the truth?

Looking at her silent, watchful cat—who had more or less turned himself into a tactful statue while Wolfe had been in the room—Storm heard herself murmur, "I should tell him the truth, shouldn't I?"

Bear sneezed, which was his way of expressing a negative opinion, and Storm sighed tiredly. He was right. She couldn't do that. But it would have been so easy. All she really had to do was to tell Wolfe calmly not to worry about the phone patch; the tap only looked as if it went into a phone line. That was how it was supposed to look.

She should know, after all.

It was her handiwork.

Four

By the time Morgan stopped by the computer room to collect her for lunch, Storm had herself well in hand. Years of practice had taught her how to present a certain face and attitude to the world no matter how she was feeling; it was an ability she needed very much at the moment. Whatever her private concerns or hurts, she preferred to deal with them alone.

She enjoyed the lunch, encouraging Morgan's talkative disposition during the meal so that she found out a great deal about the museum and its inhabitants—and wouldn't have to say very much about herself. Storm wasn't a secretive person by nature, but since she did tend to listen more than she talked, it was never difficult to keep her thoughts to herself.

When they returned to the museum, Morgan went briefly to her office and then joined Storm in the computer room. "If now's a good time to go over the security gadgets installed for the exhibit," she said, "let's do it. Unless I discover another problem, all the hardware's in place and all the display cases are pretty much finished. Since there aren't any workmen cluttering up the wing today—how about it?"

"Sounds good to me." Storm bent to remove a clipboard from one of the desk drawers which held a sheaf of papers all dealing specifically with the

Mysteries Past exhibit as well as the museum in general. There were several scaled-down floor plans of the various wings, enlargements of specific areas that would likely prove troublesome to security, and detailed diagrams of the all-important display cases—especially those newly built cases that would soon house the priceless Bannister collection of gold, gems, and artwork.

"Is he going?" Morgan asked in amusement, gesturing to Bear, who rode Storm's shoulder comfortably.

"Afraid so," Storm answered. "He wasn't happy about being left here alone while we had lunch, so he's sticking close. Don't worry—he'll stay on my shoulder until I lift him off."

Morgan accepted that amicably, and the two women made their way through the museum to the second-floor wing still closed to the public. There was quite a crowd attending the museum, so when Storm felt eyes watching her, there was no reason to believe it was Wolfe. Except that she knew it was him. She didn't know if it was instinct, intuition, or just an unnerving response of her body to his nearness, but she trusted the feeling. Just knowing he was watching was enough to make her heart beat faster, but she didn't attempt to locate him among the visitors.

She and Morgan passed through the thick velvet rope at the base of marble stairs, ignoring the signs forbidding the public to enter. Once they reached the top of the stairs, Morgan led the way, briskly and efficiently detailing the layout of the forthcoming exhibit.

Both women were completely businesslike, and worked well together. Storm asked very specific questions, about the location and placement of all the general security hardware—pressure plates, laser and infrared motion detectors, heat detectors, and so on—and about the specific security designed to guard the individual pieces of the collection in their various display cases.

Morgan answered promptly and concisely, having to refer to her clipboard of notes only occasionally. Her own curiosity showed when she said, "Clue me in, will you? I know all this security hardware is already hooked up, and that it can be turned on with the flick of a few switches. I also know that everything is connected to the equipment in the computer room and the security room. So your job is to put together a program to run everything?"

Storm nodded. "Right. For instance, a motion detector alarm is great, but since there are dozens of them, security could waste valuable time—without a monitoring system—while they tried to determine which one had been tripped. And if we don't know, very specifically, which security keycard is used to turn off corridor alarms, then one could probably be counterfeited to give an outsider access without alerting security. What I have to do is set up the system so that every piece of hardware works in conjunction with all the other parts *and* allows security personnel to monitor exactly what's going on.

"I also have to make every alarm location-specific, which means assigning every individual piece of security a number to mark its position. The system has to be set up so that it's so tightly interconnected there'll be no way a thief can disable *one* part without disturbing two or three other parts and setting off alarms. It also has to be virtually impossible for anyone to disable the whole system. And the closer he gets to anything of value, the tougher the system has to be."

Morgan whistled softly. "That's a lot of variables to take into account."

"Tell me about it. About three years ago I really screwed up a system. Believe it or not, I forgot to take into account the cleaning crew. They had their own security cards, just like the guards, but they naturally had to dust and polish the display cases, which were highly touch sensitive. This was in a huge jewelry store, by the way. The system went on-line just perfectly—and a bare hour after closing, alarms were going off like you wouldn't believe. It took me two days to calm everyone down and another two to incorporate that variable into the system."

Morgan grinned. "Our crew does the floors during hours, a section at a time, and comes in twice a week after closing for the rest. You *are* aware of that, I hope?"

"Definitely aware. And it's a pain to deal with. Actually, to limit risk, I'll have to set up the system so that the observing guard—who will have to be present in the room at all times—punches in a coded request at the control panel." She nodded toward the doorway of the room they were currently in, where what looked like a simple keypad was designed to be hidden inconspicuously behind a bit of molding. It was visible now, like all the control panels in the wing.

Fascinated, Morgan asked, "Then what?"

"Then the computer program will make several changes. Pressure plates, as well as the pressure sensitivity of the glass in the display cases, will be temporarily deactivated; laser and infrared motion detectors will switch to just monitor all activity rather than sound alarms—and that monitoring will be so precise we'll have a computer printout of every movement anyone in that room makes; and the internal alarms of the cases will be intensified so that the slightest touch of the contents will trigger the alarms. And, of course, all that will be observed visually by security personnel watching monitors in the security room."

Morgan frowned slightly. "For the *Mysteries Past* exhibit, we have brand-new, state-of-the-art alarm systems installed in this wing, but the rest of the museum isn't so up-to-date. Since your security system is for the entire building, you'll have to make this thing come together even with a jigsaw puzzle of different parts?"

"Yep."

"In less than two weeks?"

Solemnly Storm said, "That's why they pay me the big bucks."

"It sounds like you earn every penny." Morgan shook her head slightly.

"I do, but don't run away with the idea that what I do is impossible. I've had tougher assignments, believe me."

"If you say so." Glancing at her watch, the brunette added, "Damn, I've got to get on the phone and track down a decent gemologist."

"I thought the collection would stay in the vaults until just before the exhibit opens," Storm said in an idle voice.

Morgan nodded. "That's the plan, but I still need a gemologist fairly soon. Since the collection's been in storage for thirty years, it's going to need to be examined, all the pieces cleaned and readied for display. Plus, Wolfe says that Lloyd's wants a new appraisal prior to the exhibit opening. Which means I either have to find an extremely talented gemologist able to provide an appraisal *and* get the collection ready for display, or else find two different people with specialties."

"That makes sense. Well, good luck."

"Thanks. If you need any more information about the exhibit or whatever, I'll be in my office." Morgan hesitated, then said in an innocent tone, "The best person to take you over the rest of the museum's security is, of course, Wolfe. Even though it isn't really his responsibility, he made it his business to know everything about the current system. So he knows more than anyone else here, I expect."

Storm was well aware of that. Maintaining her calm, she said, "So I've heard. If you see him on the way back to your office, do you mind telling him I could use his help? I'll be on this level, north wing—with the paintings."

"My pleasure. Oh, and be sure to check out that big painting in the smaller gallery, will you? It's near the door."

"Check it out? Why?"

"You'll understand when you see it."

Storm was left somewhat puzzled, but when she made her way through the second floor into the north wing—the *Mysteries Past* exhibit was to be housed in the west wing—it didn't take her long to find the painting in question. And it was immediately apparent to her that Morgan's sense of humor was showing.

For something that had been painted hundreds of years earlier, it was curiously apt. Beneath violently stormy skies and dark clouds split open by a bolt of lightning, a lean gray wolf hunted on the edge of a forest. The animal had his back to the lightning, and so couldn't have known he was about to be struck.

Storm wondered if Wolfe had seen it.

Deciding not to draw his attention to it, she made her way into the larger of the three galleries making up the wing and began to study the security precautions. As Morgan had said, all the building except for the second-floor west wing was hampered by an outdated system, consisting mostly of old video cameras and a few newer laser grids. The paintings in this wing were, naturally, wired to alarms, just as display cases throughout the museum were, but there was as yet no overall system to coordinate everything.

Storm was standing in one of the galleries marking the placement of video cameras on the corresponding floor plan she had on her clipboard when she sensed more than heard someone come up behind her. Despite the fact that several visitors to the museum had wandered by her in the last minutes, she knew it was Wolfe, and spoke to him without turning around.

"With the new software in place, the gaps in all this old hardware are really going to show. They need more than video cameras and a few laser grids."

"I know," he said without expression. "But it would cost a fortune for the museum to upgrade. They can't afford it, at least not now. Maybe if *Mysteries Past* brings in enough revenue, they'll be able to swing it in the next year or two."

Despite his calm voice she was completely aware that he was more than a little tense; she could feel it. That was an encouragement to the reckless part of her, but a warning sign to her sensible and cautious side.

Storm studied the wall nearest her, ignoring the paintings because she was looking for something else. To Wolfe she said, "The grids are activated after hours, true?"

"Yeah."

"So whenever the guards have to traverse a corridor, they use keycards to shut the grid off until they pass through."

"Right."

She made several notations on the floor plan for the room, then turned and went back to the doorway, where she stood eyeing the gallery thoughtfully. She still didn't look at Wolfe even though she could feel his gaze on her, and she kept her voice tranquil when she spoke. "Every laser port is so visible they might as well have hung up signs."

"I know that."

Storm's keen ears caught the slight change in his deep voice. Good—she was beginning to annoy him with her businesslike attitude. Fixing him with a bland stare, she said, "If I'm going to get the new system written and on-line as quickly as possible, I need to go over the security hardware throughout the building. Morgan took me through the west wing; you seem to be the accepted expert on the rest. If you have the time, I'd like to get it done today."

He could hardly refuse, and they both knew it. So he merely nodded, said, "Tell me what you need to know," and followed her from the gallery.

For the next three hours Storm kept their pace brisk enough to try the stamina of a marathon runner. It was a very big building, and if she didn't examine every inch, she certainly went over it foot by foot. She wasted no words, asking brief questions and not encouraging anything but terse replies in return.

It wasn't the first time Wolfe had been thrown off balance by her, but it was really beginning to bother him. The sensual woman who had looked at him with passion-glazed emerald eyes only hours before seemed to have vanished, and it drove him crazy wondering if he could get her back by taking Storm in his arms. Or had that woman disappeared for good, driven away by his refusal to offer her any assurance at all that he wanted more than a warm body in his bed?

She held that damned clipboard like a shield and barely looked at him at all, speaking to him as little as possible. Wolfe wanted to . . . What? He wasn't even sure what he wanted, except her. He wanted her and couldn't have her, and the frustration of that inescapable fact was like pressure building inside him.

Dammit, he couldn't even yell at her to relieve some of the pressure. She wasn't goading him, for one thing, and besides, how could a man yell at a little blond woman with a little blond cat on her shoulder?

He couldn't accuse her of deliberately tormenting him with this cool, businesslike attitude. She was certainly capable of the tactic, he thought, but he hadn't learned how to read her well enough to know if that was her intention. It was another maddening point that she seemed to know precisely which buttons to push to get a response from him while at the same time preserving her own mysteries without effort.

He couldn't figure her out, that was the problem. She looked like such an unthreatening little thing, a pint-sized Southern lady with a drawl and wild blond hair and intense green eyes and a habit of saying things that—at the very least—disturbed his peace. She made him question himself, forced him to examine his feelings and beliefs despite his reluctance to do so.

Watching her now, as she moved faster than she talked, graceful and alert, getting her work accomplished without a wasted motion, carrying her silent little cat on her shoulder and a clipboard in one hand, he found himself—as usual—fascinated and annoyed, attracted and wary, baffled and aroused.

When it occurred to Wolfe that he'd known her a bare twenty-four hours, it was a shock.

It was nearly five o'clock, and they were alone since most of the visitors seemed to have left the museum. They had reached the final area, the south wing, first floor, where the museum's existing gem collection was housed, and no one else was anywhere to be seen. This area, which had been the target of a thief not so long ago, was only a bit better protected than the rest, boasting display cases that were, Storm said, "slightly younger than God."

It wasn't the first disparaging comment she'd made during the afternoon, but it was the first in more than an hour, and it gave Wolfe an opportunity to vent some of the pressure building up inside him.

"Don't be so condescending," he snapped, relieved to have something to get mad about.

Storm rounded on him as if she'd been waiting for the same opportunity herself. They were no more than a couple of feet apart, so she had to tilt her head back a little to meet his angry gaze. Despite that, it was obvious she didn't feel the slightest bit dismayed by his greater size or by his anger.

"Who, me?" Her drawl was, in some manner Wolfe couldn't define, peculiarly cutting.

"Yes, you. You haven't missed a chance to ridicule the security in this building."

"That's probably because there isn't any. You want to tell me how the hell I'm supposed to design a system to protect this building when ten-year-old laser grids are expected to function side by side with pressure alarms older than I am? Older than you are, for that matter."

That last mocking remark nearly surprised a laugh out of him, but he managed to bite it back. Using a bit of sarcasm himself, he said, "Hey, you're the one who seemed to think this would be a piece of cake, genius. I haven't heard anybody else call it easy, so I doubt you were lured here with false promises."

"I wasn't lured anywhere," she said, the clipboard tucked under one arm and both hands planted on her hips. "I was sent here to do a job, which I will do. Nobody promised me a thing, false or otherwise, except my usual pay. And a bonus if I could get along with you."

For a minute Wolfe thought she was serious. Given his past communications with Ace Security, which could best be termed acrimonious, it wouldn't have been all that surprising. But then he saw the gleam of amusement in her green eyes, and he realized she was pulling his leg. A split second later he realized something else.

"You've been goading me all afternoon, haven't you?" he demanded. "Ridiculing the security here because you knew it'd make me mad."

"Something like that," she murmured.

"Why?"

Storm was smiling slightly. "You've been very tense. I thought it might help if you could let off a little steam."

Wolfe drew a breath. "I see." Dammit, she was still pushing buttons—and all the right ones too. Worse, she was reading him like a book written in that easy-on-the-eyes crystal-clear type. And worse yet, she was so nonchalant about his temper that she was perfectly willing to incite him to lose it.

None of which seemed to have any effect whatsoever on the fact that he wanted her more with every minute that passed. It was enough to drive a man crazy.

"Tell me something. Where did your mother get the name Wolfe?"

He blinked at the abrupt change of subject. "What makes you think my mother came up with the name?" he asked, drawn away from his irate thoughts totally against his will.

"Instinct. Or intuition maybe. I doubt a man would have picked the name unless it was a family tradition—and with Nickerson tacked on, I kind of doubt that's the case."

He still wasn't sure where this was going, but had to smile. "You're right. Wolfe was Mother's choice. She said it was because of my eyes. When I was old enough to consider the matter, I pointed out that most infants had blue eyes—and wolves usually don't. She said it had nothing to do with color." He shrugged. "Beats the hell out of me."

Storm understood completely. And she wished she could meet Wolfe's mother; any woman who could gaze into the infant eyes of her son and see the seeds of the formidable man he would one day become was a woman well worth knowing.

And, Storm recalled, she had named her older son Maxim, which was short for Maximilian and which meant something along the lines of "greatest in excellence." Max Bannister had been born into wealth, but had his mother realized from the beginning that her son would one day become known less for his wealth than for his kind heart and caring nature?

Cutting off her thoughts, Wolfe said, "How on earth did we get on the subject of my name, anyway?"

Storm looked at him for a moment, then smiled. "You were about to tense up again."

"What are you—three parts witch?" he demanded.

"Only one part. The other two parts are Irish and Cajun."

Wolfe all but winced. "If that isn't a combustible mixture, I don't know what is."

"Yeah. And you don't want to get your fingers burned."

It shouldn't have surprised him, Wolfe reflected wryly, that she would ruthlessly return them to the point where he had earlier walked out of the computer room. If he had learned nothing else about Storm Tremaine, he had learned she was utterly fearless in confronting whatever obstacle stood in her way. Even if it was him.

Carefully he said, "We ended this discussion a few hours ago."

"No, the discussion didn't end. It just stopped. Rather abruptly, as I recall."

Wolfe jammed his hands into the pockets of his jacket and settled his shoulders. It was probably better to clear the decks here, he thought, where the possibility of being interrupted at least kept him from following his instincts. Despite all his rational misgivings he could barely think about anything except how much he wanted her.

"All right then," he said grimly. "We'll finish it. I'm not about to lie and say I don't want you; we both know better. But I'm also old enough to have learned that it isn't going to kill me if I don't get what I want. You pointed out something along those lines yourself."

Storm regarded him thoughtfully. She was getting herself into more trouble than she needed, and she knew it, but she couldn't seem to stop herself. So it didn't really surprise her when she heard herself say, "Let me get this straight. You want me—and heaven knows I've offered—but it isn't going to happen because I asked for one small assurance you can't—or won't—give?"

He nodded, silent.

Very softly she said, "Some women need promises, Wolfe. Even if they're only lies."

"I'm not going to lie to you." He kept his voice even.

At least not about this, she thought. And she wondered if that should be her guideline as well; even if part of her life was filled with lies, she could keep this part honest. Couldn't she? Or would Wolfe hate her even more when he discovered the truth about her?

For an instant Storm wavered. But looking at him, overwhelmingly conscious of the unexpected strength of her own desire, she silently gave up the struggle. There would be time later to count the cost; for now, she felt an enormous relief in having made the decision.

With a faint smile she said, "We all pay prices for what we want, don't we? I'm willing to set aside all those quaint, old-fashioned ideas drummed into me since childhood, throw myself into a brief affair knowing it won't lead to the altar—and I'll pay a price for that. But I'm not asking anything of you except one small assurance that I'll be a little more than another notch on your bedpost."

"I don't do that," he said tightly.

"Oh, sure you do, Wolfe. Not literally—at least, I suppose not—but you must be keeping count. There wouldn't have been so many if the number didn't matter."

That gave him a very sobering shock—because she just might be right. Before he could react, she was going on in the same quiet drawl, the tone matter-of-fact.

"Anyway, my point is that I can only meet you halfway. No matter which way you look at it, I'm giving up a lot more than you are, so I'll be damned if I give up my pride as well."

"You make it sound like a battle," he said.

Her smile turned a bit rueful. "It probably will be, considering the sparks we strike off each other. But I'd prefer to look on it as a kind of grand adventure." She hesitated, then added, "One I've never had before."

Wolfe forced himself to wait a moment so that he wouldn't blurt out the question. Slowly he said, "Are you saying what I think you're saying?"

Characteristically Storm answered bluntly and with a total lack of self-consciousness. "That you'd be the first man in my bed? Yes, that's what I'm saying."

"How old are you?" he demanded.

"Pushing thirty," she said promptly, then chuckled. "Well, twenty-eight, anyway. Naturally, being a proud woman, I have to assure you that there *have* been offers in the past."

"I don't doubt it."

Storm eyed him, decided that he was still somewhat stunned by her revelation, and kept talking to give him time to pull himself together.

"Of course, I had boyfriends in high school and college, and the pressure got a bit intense from time to time, but I was never really tempted to experiment. I suppose I just wasn't ready. And with six older brothers, all a bit fierce about their baby sister, nobody pushed me too hard." She shrugged. "Then, after school, my career was—is—pretty demanding. Till you stalked into my life yesterday, I still wasn't tempted."

Wolfe cleared his throat and forced a note of mockery. "Then you took one look and tumbled, huh?"

Storm laughed. "Something like that."

He stared at her, his awareness of everything but her fading into the background. She hadn't changed position all during their conversation, so she was still standing with her hands on her hips, chin raised to meet his eyes; even with her casual clothing, a clipboard under one arm and a cat on her shoulder half-hidden by wild blond hair, she was incredibly sexy.

It was difficult to believe she could be a virgin—but not impossible. As forthright and self-confident as she was, he hadn't needed to be told that sex was something she would make up her mind about based on her own beliefs and judgments and regardless of peer pressure. It was just astonishing to him that in the years since school there had apparently been no man able to change her mind.

Until he had "stalked" into her life yesterday.

Fighting a silent battle with himself, Wolfe said, "If you've waited this long, why settle for an affair?"

Storm looked faintly surprised. "I haven't been *waiting*, not the way you seem to mean. Despite my upbringing it wasn't fixed in my head it had to be marriage or nothing; I'm a bit too independent by nature to think that way. In fact, I like my life just fine as is, without the encumbrance of a husband—or lover." She shrugged. "Maybe that's why the timing's right now; because I want a man who doesn't want ties. Looks to me like it suits us both. In a few weeks I'll be on my way again, free as when I got here."

"And me?"

"You too. No demands, no complications, no hurts—no problems. Just what I trust will be a pleasant memory for both of us."

Wolfe knew he'd be a fool to turn her down. There had been a few similar offers in the past, which he had promptly accepted and for which he felt no regrets. But Storm . . . Every instinct warned him that, with Storm, there could never be anything simple and uncomplicated, least of all an affair. She was too complex and her effect on him was too unexpectedly intense to allow for simplicity.

And she was a virgin. He thought of that, thought of being the first man in her bed, watching her learn the secrets of passion for the first time, and the surge of raw desire he felt very nearly got the better of him.

"No," he said harshly.

She didn't flinch at his tone, or appear the slightest bit ruffled by the rejection. In fact, she smiled at him, and her drawling voice remained casual and matter-of-fact.

"Maybe I should have warned you about the Tremaines. We don't give up so easily."

Wolfe didn't say a word when she turned and headed briskly for the computer room. And he didn't move. He just stood there, surrounded by lighted display cases of gems in a virtually silent museum, and he would have sworn he could see the gauntlet flung down on the marble floor in front of him.

As she neared the computer room Storm's steps slowed and she drew a deep breath.

"Yaaa," Bear murmured in her ear.

She released the breath. "Shut up. I've burned my bridges."

Refusing to think about anything, she called for a cab as soon as she got to her desk, then gathered up what she needed to take back to her hotel and left, locking the door behind her. It wasn't yet six o'clock, but since she planned to work in her suite, she didn't feel guilty about leaving early.

No one could have said Storm bolted from the museum, but she didn't waste any time in leaving. Making a mental note to rent that Jeep she'd mentioned to Wolfe, she paid the cab in front of her hotel and went up to the suite. She dumped everything she was carrying onto the couch, including Bear, and immediately sat down to wrestle her boots off.

Half an hour later she was comfortably dressed in an old, frayed sweater and leggings and was curled up on the couch. She had a meeting later—not here as before, because he was wary of being seen here too many times—and her supper was on its way up from room service. She turned on the television, more to provide background noise than anything else, and began sorting through her notes and diagrams.

She tried not to think about Wolfe, but his face kept intruding on her thoughts. Those eyes of his, so fiercely blue, seemed burned in her memory, like the sharp angle of his jaw and the curve of his sensual lips.

Burned, like her bridges. There was no going back now, she knew. Impossible to turn around, even if she'd wanted to. She was following her heart, allowing it to lead her even though her head told her she was likely to regret it. But Storm could only do her best. With all the lies in her life, her only choice was to pick a dividing line and stick to it. It was a chancy decision, and she knew it, but she didn't really have a choice.

Because of a promise given, she couldn't tell Wolfe the whole truth, and because of what she had come here to do, he was the last man on earth she should have gotten involved with on any personal level—least of all an intimate one.

It wasn't until much later that evening, when she was on her way to the meeting, that the real crux of the matter became clear in Storm's mind. The simple truth was, she was caught between two very strong-willed men, bound to obey one—and seemingly fated to fall in love with the other.

Five

It was nearly midnight when Wolfe caught himself pacing his comfortable apartment for at least the third time since he'd arrived home at eleven. After leaving the museum just minutes after Storm had—that information courtesy of one of the guards—he'd returned to his apartment long enough to change and then gone on to a party he'd been invited to weeks before.

He had spent the evening being uncomfortably aware that his date—a five-foot-nine-inch blond former model named Cyndy—exactly matched Storm's mocking description of Barbie dolls. The glossy blonde with the accentless, almost toneless voice knew jewelry because she wore a ton of it and because her father owned the largest retail jewelry business in the city, but other than that they had absolutely nothing in common.

Wolfe cut the evening short, explaining that he had to make an overseas call—which wasn't a lie—and left Cyndy at her door despite her invitation to make his call from her bedroom phone. Even though he was familiar with the room in question, he felt no temptation to take Cyndy up on her offer. Which was yet another sobering realization.

So he came home alone and got out of his tux, so restless he couldn't be still for long, his thoughts jumbled. For one of the very few times in his adult life, he found it almost impossible to concentrate on his work, even though that had been the focus of his life *and* his emotional anchor for nearly fifteen years. But now it seemed clear that Storm had gotten under his skin so deeply, even the panacea of his job had no power to dislodge her.

He was wavering and he knew it. He wanted her too much to be able to ignore the offer she'd made, no matter how much the prospect of any kind of commitment alarmed him. That was his problem—his desire was pulling him in one direction while his caution held on to him with sharp talons.

The truth was, she *did* mean more to him than a mere physical conquest, and he knew there was no way he would be satisfied with a few brief nights in her bed—but he didn't want to admit that to Storm. It was why he had backed away, not because he was unable to give her the assurances she asked for, but because he was unwilling. Maybe it was his pride that made him reluctant to admit she had gotten to him so completely, but there was more to it than simple ego, he thought.

There was also Storm. She deserved more than she was asking for, for one thing. A lot more. He knew in his bones she did. Dammit, she *deserved* to expect those "quaint, old-fashioned" notions of love and marriage to be promised to her.

It struck Wolfe as ironically amusing that he of all men would feel so strongly about the subject. He'd certainly never thought about it with other women. But Storm was different from any woman he'd ever known. She was a woman who was designed—by nature or simply by her own life experiences—to walk by a man's side as his equal and companion, to be his partner in life, not just his lover in bed; to ask her to be anything less would be to threaten her spirit.

Even more, Wolfe knew that her effect on him was hardly something to be taken lightly. The kind of strength she had would always mark a man in some way, change him forever, no matter how much he thought himself master of the situation. All his instincts told him she was a woman who would carve a place for herself in a man's heart, with him for the rest of his life, as unforgettable as his own name.

And that, he told himself repeatedly, was not something he was ready for.

It was nearly midnight when he sat down to make his call, forcing himself to concentrate on business. The number he called was a familiar one, a special private line to an office in Paris. He waited for the connection to be made, slightly impatient because it took longer than usual. When the receiver was finally picked up, the deep voice sounded very harassed— and very French even though it only snapped a one-word name.

"Chavalier."

"If your mood's that rotten," Wolfe said, "I'll call back some other time."

"Nothing's wrong with my mood," Jared Chavalier said, now sounding no more French than Wolfe did. "It's the rest of the world causing problems."

Wolfe grunted. "Know what you mean. Listen, can you do me a favor?"

"I suppose you want me to check Interpol's files for information of some kind, as usual?"

"Yeah. Max's exhibit is due to open in just a few weeks now, and I'm trying to anticipate problems."

"Okay," Jared said, "what do you need from me?"

"Two things. I have a few questions about one of our local collectors, and I'd appreciate any information you can dig up. Her name's Nyssa Armstrong." He spelled the name briskly, adding her address.

"Got it. And the second thing?"

Wolfe hesitated, then said, "I'm a little worried about the security company we're using. Max still has faith in them, but after the first technician they sent us screwed up, I started to wonder. And since I've seen Nyssa coming out of their offices here in the city—when I happen to know she uses a different security company herself—I can't help but be concerned. At the very least the company seems too damned prone to leaking information. Their reputation is excellent, but I'd like to know more than what I've found in the public record." He named Ace Security, provided the address and other necessary information, and said, "See what you can find out about the outfit. All right?"

"No problem. It may take a few days, though. I have to use the computer on a time-sharing basis, remember, and this isn't exactly official business."

"Yeah, I know. The collection isn't threatened until we take it out of the vaults, so I have some time before the information's critical. Just let me know."

"All right."

When he cradled the receiver a few minutes later, Wolfe rose to his feet and went to the living-room window. The apartment boasted a fairly spectacular view of the San Francisco Bay, and in the daylight it was possible to see either a fog bank or the Golden Gate Bridge—whichever happened to be visible. But right now what Wolfe saw were the multicolored lights of the city, some of them hazy because a light fog was rolling in.

He wanted to continue thinking of business, but as he idly watched the lights and the fog his thoughts returned to Storm. Her hotel wasn't very far away. In fact, if he went and looked out his bedroom window, he could see it.

He was almost tempted to pick up the phone again and call her, just to hear the lazy drawl of her voice, but he resisted the urge. She had the trick of throwing him off balance, of maneuvering him, and it was that more than anything else that he was wary of. No matter what happened next in their relationship, he wanted to make damned sure he had at least some control over his own choices.

For a long time after he hung up the phone, Jared Chavalier stared down at the notes he'd made while talking to Wolfe. Then he sighed, tore off the top page of the pad, crumpled it up, and threw it somewhat viciously toward a nearby trash can. It missed, which didn't improve his mood.

He got up and went to a window, gazing out without paying much attention to what he saw. His eyes moved restlessly though, scanning the horizon even while his mind was occupied with methodical thoughts.

"Damn," he murmured finally. He took a good look at the view then, noting that the fog was thickening, blotting out the lights of the bridge. It looked miserable out there, and for a moment he wished he were back in Paris. He muttered another curse, then returned to the spindly desk his hotel provided. He didn't pick up the special phone, the one that would accept only calls routed through his Paris office. Instead he picked up the standard hotel phone.

When his call was answered, he didn't offer a greeting, but simply said, "We've got a problem."

For the next two days Storm barely saw Wolfe. She didn't go out of her way to see him, biding her time patiently and allowing her work to occupy her. In truth, because she was on such a short schedule, the project filled more than her usual working hours, and she always spent at least several hours in her hotel suite each evening going over plans, diagrams, operation manuals dealing with the security hardware, and her notes as she planned a rather involved computer program.

By Friday afternoon she had begun writing the program, filling the first sheet of a brand-new legal pad with line after line of precise mathematical formulas. She expected to take another three or four days to finish writing the program and go over it for possible problems, though there would likely be a few bugs showing up only after the program was installed and running. There usually were.

The work occupied her thoughts and attention, for which she was grateful, but it didn't do much to help her sleep. She was acclimated by now, the jet lag past, but dreaming about Wolfe had become a habit that left her nights somewhat disturbed. Even Bear had taken to napping often during the day—a feline habit but not one of his—because she kept him awake tossing and turning half the night.

The situation might have continued indefinitely—since Wolfe was a stubborn man and since Storm was still worried about gaining his trust under false pretenses—but the status quo was disturbed late Friday afternoon when a visitor came into the museum.

"Hi, there."

Storm looked up, startled, to see Nyssa Armstrong standing just inside the doorway of the computer room. The older woman, polished and sophisticated in a silk dress with her pale gold hair bound up in a refined chignon, makeup perfect, and bland social smile on her precisely painted lips, made Storm feel instantly threatened—and that reaction had nothing at all to do with business.

In a contest of elegance, Nyssa won hands down. Storm was dressed with her usual casual indifference in faded jeans, boots, and a thick green sweater about two sizes too big for her. In addition, her hair was full of static electricity today, there was a smudge of ink on her nose, a pencil tucked behind each ear, and she had chewed one thumbnail down to a nub.

For one awful moment Storm couldn't help wondering what on earth made her even imagine that Wolfe could possibly prefer her to someone like this sleek creature. And if the memory of his desire was reassuring, the fact that he'd avoided her for the past two days wasn't.

Highly conscious of her own disheveled state, Storm was nonetheless concerned first with security. She rose to her feet, smoothly turning the legal pad on which she'd been working face-down, and went around the desk to face the other woman.

"Ms. Armstrong, you shouldn't be back here," she said mildly. "Didn't one of the guards stop you?" Wolfe had posted a guard at the end of the hallway of offices the day after Storm had told him about the phone patch.

Nyssa widened her blue eyes innocently. "Oh, he let me pass. I've been here several times to visit Max— and Wolfe, of course. The guards know me."

Storm made a rather grim mental note to do something about *that.* "I see. Well, since you're here—what can I do for you?" She stood in such a way as to prevent Nyssa from coming farther into the room.

"Actually I came to see Wolfe. You don't mind, do you, dear?"

For a full minute Storm didn't trust herself to speak. First of all, she disliked being called *dear,* especially by another woman and most especially by a woman she'd encountered only once before in her life—and then in the ladies' room of a restaurant. She also had no trouble whatsoever deducing the fact that Nyssa was bent on making trouble.

Pleasantly Storm said, "Why ask me? Whatever's between you and Wolfe is entirely your own business. But his office is down the hall, you know."

In a voice every bit as spuriously polite as Storm's, Nyssa said, "No, I didn't know that. I've never actually been in his office, you see."

"Then I'd be happy to show you," Storm said, all but nudging the other woman back out into the hall so she could close the door to the computer room. "This way."

"You have such a lovely accent," Nyssa said, following Storm. "Georgia? Alabama?"

"Louisiana." Storm happened to know Wolfe was presently in his office, because she'd seen him go past her door nearly an hour before. So she rapped sharply on the door, opened it, said, "You have a visitor," and motioned Nyssa inside before Wolfe could even begin to rise from his chair.

She didn't wait to see what reaction Nyssa would be greeted with, but closed the door and turned to go back to her own bailiwick. It didn't much surprise her to find Morgan waiting at the door of her own office—a door that had been closed when Storm had led Nyssa past it.

Leaning against her doorjamb, Morgan said gravely, "I see she's hunting again."

Storm paused and considered the matter. "Looks that way," she allowed.

"And that doesn't bother you?"

"Why should it? Except for the fact that she has the eyes of a serial killer, I'd say she's perfect for him."

Morgan lost her solemnity as she grinned. "Meow."

Storm felt a smile tugging at her own lips. "Okay, so the woman gets on my nerves."

"I'm glad to hear you've got nerves. I was beginning to wonder. And I certainly hope you mean to do something about Nyssa's blatant attempt to get her claws into Wolfe."

"He's a big boy. He can take care of himself."

"Yes, but that's hardly the point, is it?" Morgan's amber eyes were gleaming.

Storm shook her head. "Her primary interest is the exhibit, and we both know it. Taking Wolfe away from me—if that's what she imagines she's doing—is nothing more than a pleasant diversion for her."

Morgan nodded, grave again. "True, very true. So it doesn't bother you a bit, huh?"

"Not a bit."

"Uh-huh. So why're your hands clenched into fists?"

Storm looked down and made a conscious effort to relax her hands. It was surprisingly difficult. She flexed her fingers and cleared her throat. "I'm a little tense. Big deal." She squared her shoulders determinedly. "It's been a long day. I think I'll pick up all my toys and go home now."

"And if Wolfe should ask?"

"What makes you think he would?"

"Probably because he's been more than a little edgy lately when he doesn't know where you are," Morgan reflected. "He usually asks me or one of the guards. When you vanished at lunchtime yesterday, I thought he was going to drive us all crazy prowling around until you came back."

A little blankly Storm said, "I didn't see him when I came in."

"No, I imagine he made sure you didn't."

This was very interesting, but Storm mentally allowed a bit of room for exaggeration; Morgan wouldn't do it consciously, but since she was clearly rooting for a relationship between Wolfe and Storm, she could have allowed wishful thinking to cloud her otherwise clear perceptions.

"He won't ask," Storm said.

"Oh, I think he will."

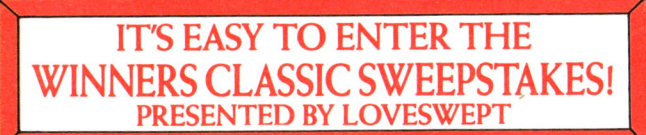

IT'S EASY TO ENTER THE WINNERS CLASSIC SWEEPSTAKES!
PRESENTED BY LOVESWEPT

Where will Passion lead you?

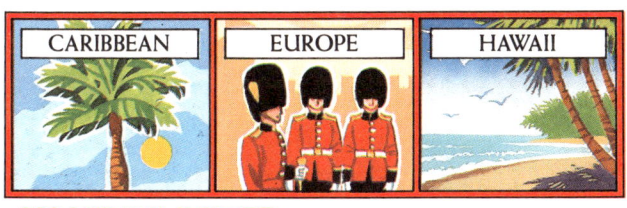

| CARIBBEAN | EUROPE | HAWAII |

YOU'RE INVITED

to enter our Winners Classic Sweepstakes presented by Loveswept for a chance to win a romantic 14-day vacation for two to Hawaii, Europe or the Caribbean ...PLUS $5,000 CASH!

Don't break our heart!

FREE ENTRY! **FREE BOOKS!**

Peel off both halves of this heart and unite them on the Entry Form enclosed. Use both halves to get the most from this special offer.

SPECIAL BONUS:

Get 6 FREE Loveswept books, *plus* another wonderful gift just for trying Loveswept Romances. See details inside...

WIN THE ROMANTIC VACATION OF A LIFETIME...
PLUS $5000 SPENDING MONEY!

Take your pick — Hawaii, Europe or the Caribbean — and enjoy 14 passion-filled days and sultry nights if you're the winner of the Winners Classic Sweepstakes presented by Loveswept. It's *free* to enter, so don't miss out!

YOU COULD WIN YOUR DREAM TRIP!

Just peel off the FREE ENTRY side of our bright red heart, and place it on the Entry Form to the right. But don't stop there!

...AND GET LOVESWEPT EVERY MONTH!

Use the FREE BOOKS sticker and you'll get your first shipment of 6 Loveswept Romance books absolutely free! PLUS, we'll sign you up for the most romantic book service in the world! About once a month you get 6 new Loveswept novels. You always get 15 days to examine the books, and if you decide to keep them, you'll get 6 books for the price of 5! Be the first to thrill to these new stories. Your Loveswept books will always arrive before they're available in any store. There's no minimum. You can cancel at anytime by simply writing "cancel" on your invoice and returning the books to us. We'll pay the postage. So try the Loveswept romantic book service today!

Get a FREE heart-pendant necklace and 6 free Loveswept books!

This elegant heart-pendant is etched with delicate, smaller hearts and, along with its 18" chain, is gold-plated to retain an exquisite beauty for many years to come.

BOTH GIFTS ARE YOURS TO KEEP NO MATTER WHAT!

DON'T HOLD BACK!

1. No obligation! No purchase necessary! Enter our Sweepstakes for a chance to win!
2. FREE! Get your first shipment of 6 Loveswept books *and* a heart-pendant necklace as free gifts.
3. Save money! Become a member and about once a month you get 6 books for the price of 5! Return any shipment you don't want.
4. Be the first! You'll always receive your Loveswept books before they are available in stores. You'll be the first to thrill to these exciting new stories.

WINNERS CLASSIC SWEEPSTAKES
Entry Form

YES! I want to see where passion will lead me!

Place FREE ENTRY Sticker Here

Place FREE BOOKS Sticker Here

Enter me in the sweepstakes! I have placed my FREE ENTRY sticker on the heart.

Send me six *free* Loveswept novels *and* my *free* necklace! I have placed my FREE BOOKS sticker on the heart.

Mend a broken heart. Use both stickers to get the most from this special offer!

61259

NAME_____

ADDRESS_____ APT._____

CITY_____

STATE_____ ZIP_____

Loveswept's Heartfelt Promise to You!

There's no purchase necessary to enter the sweepstakes. There is no obligation to buy when you send for your free books and heart-pendant necklace. You may preview each new shipment for 15 days free. If you decide against it, simply return the shipment within 15 days and owe nothing. If you keep them, pay only $2.25 per book — a savings of 54¢ per book (plus postage & handling, and sales tax in NY and Canada.) Prices subject to change. Orders subject to approval. See complete sweepstakes rules at the back of this book.

CB

Give in to love and see where passion leads you!
Enter the Winners Classic Sweepstakes and
send for your FREE heart-pendant necklace
and 6 FREE Loveswept books today!
(See details inside.)

BUSINESS REPLY MAIL
FIRST-CLASS MAIL   PERMIT NO. 2456   HICKSVILLE, NY

POSTAGE WILL BE PAID BY ADDRESSEE

Loveswept

Bantam Doubleday Dell Direct, Inc.
P.O. Box 985
Hicksville, NY 11802-9827

NO POSTAGE
NECESSARY
IF MAILED
IN THE
UNITED STATES

Detach here and mail today.

She didn't think he would, but Storm felt a burst of recklessness seize her. "If he should ask, you can tell him I said he'd better watch the pillow talk with Nyssa. I'd hate to have to change the computer access codes."

Morgan's eyes grew huge. "Are you sure you want me to tell him that?"

"Why not?"

"Oh, no reason. I suppose you know what you're doing."

Privately Storm doubted it, but she wasn't about to back down. "Certainly I do. See you Monday."

"I hope so."

Storm's vast irritation carried her through the next hour in fine style. She gathered up the work she meant to do over the weekend, picked up Bear, and went out to the parking lot where her rented Jeep waited. When she got to her hotel suite, she dumped everything and immediately went to take a shower, trusting to lots of hot water to ease the tension she felt.

It only half worked, but that was enough to make her laugh ruefully at herself as she dried her hair a few minutes later. Since he'd avoided her for the past two days, she figured Wolfe wouldn't be interested enough in her whereabouts to ask Morgan—no matter what the brunette thought—so the really nasty message calculated to enrage him had been wasted. And her anger at Nyssa was fairly useless; she'd encountered enough women like the older blonde to have learned that the sleek, polished surface of them was like armor.

The realizations left Storm feeling slightly drained and more than a little depressed. She changed into one of her comfortable working ensembles, this one made up of a flannel-lined but silky looking black top and leggings that resembled pajamas, and a pair of thin black socks because her feet were cold.

She turned the television on to a news program and was just about to find the room-service menu when a sudden pounding on the door made her jump. It didn't take a lot of imagination to figure out who the visitor was, and Storm wasn't sure how she felt about it as she went to open the door.

It was Wolfe, and she'd never seen him so mad.

"May I come in?" he asked with exquisite politeness.

She stepped back and allowed him to pass, then shut the door and followed him into the living area. In her best damn-the-torpedoes tone of voice she said, "You must have gotten my message."

Wolfe had shrugged out of his black jacket in the gesture of a man who wanted to be prepared for anything, and tossed it over the back of the couch—narrowly missing Bear, who hunkered down and watched silently.

"Yes, I did, and what the *hell* did you mean by it?" Wolfe snapped, glaring at her.

Since she was wearing only socks, he towered over her by more than a foot, and rage came off him in waves so strong they were practically visible, but Storm didn't back down or back away; it simply wasn't in her. Taking up for herself as a child with six older brothers to torment her—all of whom were considerably larger than her—had taught her not to give an inch of ground willingly.

She planted her hands on her hips, raised her chin so her eyes met his dangerous ones, and snapped right back at him. "I thought my meaning was perfectly clear. But if you want words of one syllable, I'll give them to you."

"What I want is a damned apology. You had no business saying that—and to Morgan, for God's sake. It'll be all over the city by Monday—"

"Like it isn't already? Listen, if you think for one minute that Nyssa's plans for you are secret—think again. You're already party gossip in this city, hero.

She's got you on her hook. And from what I hear, Nyssa hasn't lost one yet."

"I am not on her hook!" he yelled. "Dammit, I *told* you she didn't get what she wanted from me. I wouldn't give her first look at the collection no matter what she offered, and if you believe differently . . ."

"Yeah, what?"

Wolfe made a visible effort to calm down, and when he spoke again, his voice was more controlled. "You honestly think I'd give in to her? Even worse—you think I'd give away security secrets or even useless information as payback for a good time in bed? That's what you think of me?"

"What I think? I think you could give stubborn lessons to a jackass," she snapped.

He stared at her. "Is this the same fight we started a minute ago?"

"No, it's a different one."

She was trying to knock him off balance again, he decided, and it made him even madder. "I don't want to start a new fight until the old one's finished. Are you going to apologize for what you said, or not?"

"Not." She lifted her chin an inch higher. "So that finishes the first fight."

On some level of his mind, it occurred to Wolfe that absurdity went a long way toward defusing anger, but he was still mad enough not to recognize that their fight was beginning to lean in a comical direction. He was so mad he was almost shaking; he wanted to yell and destroy things. Unfortunately the focus of his rage was a tiny blonde—even smaller without her boots than he was accustomed to—who could give a few lessons in stubbornness to donkeys herself, and who he couldn't have lifted a hand against no matter how furious he was.

She stood there glaring at him, her small, expressive face angry and her green eyes bright with temper, and he knew that no matter how much he raged, she wasn't going to back down so much as an inch. It was maddening.

"Oh, hell," he muttered. "What's the second fight about?" The question didn't strike him as at all ridiculous at the time, though it would later.

"Your stubbornness."

"Look who's talking."

"Me, stubborn? I'm not stubborn. I'm just right."

Wolfe felt them drifting off track again, but he couldn't seem to stop it. "Right about what?"

"Your stubbornness."

"This is a ridiculous conversation," he suddenly realized.

"I'm serious," she snapped.

He stared at her. "If you expect to be taken seriously, never wear pajamas with feet in them."

Storm returned his stare for a moment, then looked down at her feet bemusedly. Then she looked back at Wolfe and burst out laughing. He found himself laughing as well, the anger gone as though it had never existed.

When she could, Storm said, "I'm not wearing pajamas with feet in them, I'm just wearing socks that happen to match my leggings." She was leaning a hip against the back of the couch, relaxed now that the confrontation was over.

"Oh. Well, they look like pajamas with feet in them."

She swallowed a chuckle as she looked at him. He was smiling at her, that utterly charming smile she hadn't seen from him in days, and she hoped it would be a long time—if ever—before he found out that he could win any argument with her by using his softer side. Even now it was almost impossible for her to think about anything except how much she wanted to be back in his arms.

Dryly she said, "Okay, I was out of line with what I said about you and Nyssa."

"Thank you," he said promptly, accepting the apology without crowing about it. "And just so you don't think I take your opinion lightly, I am checking her out."

"I thought you'd already done that," Storm murmured, unable to bite back the mild sarcasm.

"Don't start again," Wolfe warned her severely. "What I should have said is that I am *having* Nyssa Armstrong's background checked out."

"Oh." Storm looked at him thoughtfully. "By who?"

He shrugged. "I have a contact with the police. It's useful in my line of work."

"I guess it would be. So—you think she could be a threat to the collection after all?"

Wolfe hesitated, then shrugged again. "It's a possibility. She's certainly not hiding her interest. That's why she came to the museum today, by the way."

Storm smiled slightly. "You mean it was business, not personal? Think again. She came by the computer room first, remember, so I know what was on her mind. The collection, sure, but you too. She enjoys being a vamp."

"I haven't heard that word in years," Wolfe said, shaking his head.

Storm barely hesitated. "Maybe I should take a lesson from her. Much as it galls me to admit it, I seem to be a total failure as a seductress."

Wolfe knew that the sensible thing to do would be to pick up his jacket and leave. But days of frustration hadn't done anything except leave him wanting her more than ever, and not all of his rational arguments could make a dent in that desire. His feelings were far stronger than his thoughts, especially where she was concerned.

She had put him through a wringer in the last few minutes, drawing emotions from him—first rage, then humor, and now desire—and he knew his sense of control over any of it was only an illusion. All he could be certain of was his overpowering certainty that if he walked away from her this time, he would regret it for the rest of his life.

"No," he said finally, huskily. "You aren't a failure."

"More sleepless nights?" She was smiling a little, her green eyes softened.

"They're getting to be a habit. What have you done to me, Storm?"

She was silent for a moment, just looking up at him, and then she straightened away from the couch and took two small steps, exactly halving the distance between them.

Meeting him halfway.

Wolfe was never sure afterward if he made a conscious decision or if he simply obeyed an urge so inexorable he had never really had a choice to make. In any case, as if something had snapped, he closed the remaining distance between them with one step and pulled her into his arms. Storm made a little sound, her arms sliding up around his neck as she rose on her tiptoes against him and lifted her face invitingly. Wolfe didn't hesitate, pulling her even tighter against him and lowering his head to cover her soft, parted lips with his own. It shouldn't have surprised him by then, the eruption of searingly hot need that instantly blasted over them both, but the power of it still staggered him.

It was like some elemental force too-long trapped and now finally released, different from anything Wolfe had ever felt before he had met her. His hunger for her was absolute, a living thing that had to be satisfied. He could feel his heart slamming against his chest, feel the softness of her breasts pressed against it, feel the tremors that shook her delicate body, and every nerve of his own body seemed overloaded by pure, raw sensation.

His hands slid down her back to her hips, curving around the firm flesh of her bottom, lifting her against the pulsing fullness of his loins. A faint, purring sound of pleasure throbbed in her throat and her arms tightened around his neck as his long, powerful fingers held her lower body against his and kneaded sensuously.

Wolfe lifted his head finally, trying to control his ragged breathing and having no luck at all. Like the pounding of his heart, his breathing was driven wildly by this intense, escalating need. Hoarsely he said, "You aren't wearing a damn thing under these silly pajamas, are you?"

"They aren't pajamas," Storm murmured almost idly. Her eyes were sleepy with desire, her lips parted slightly, and her face was softly flushed. "And, no, I'm not wearing anything under them. You can feel that, can't you?"

He certainly could, and it was like throwing dry timber on a fire. The flimsy material between his hands and her flesh was so thin it was almost no barrier at all, but it was still too much, still an obstruction preventing him from feeling her warm skin beneath his touch. He had spent days thinking about her, imagining how her delicate body would look and feel naked, picturing her lovely face awakened in sensual pleasure, and now the reality of her in his arms was almost staggering.

He held himself still as he tried to master the fierce desire gripping his body, worried that he wanted her too much, that he might frighten or hurt her with the overwhelming force of his need. He didn't want to do anything to mar this first joining for her, no matter what it cost him, and he struggled to contain the overwhelming urgency of what he felt. But then she moved against him, innocently seductive, and Wolfe groaned aloud.

Her green eyes gleamed up at him. "I want you," she said huskily. "You aren't going to say no this time, are you? Don't say no again, Wolfe."

He had the sudden clear certainty that he would never be able to say no to her again, about anything, but he wouldn't have told her that even if he could have managed a coherent sentence. Instead he muttered something wordless and swung her up into his arms, finding her mouth again almost blindly.

He carried her into the bedroom and set her on her feet beside the wide bed. The drapes were closed and the lamp on the nightstand was burning, so it might have been any hour of the day or night, and since it was a hotel room, it was blandly decorated and impersonal, but Wolfe didn't notice any of that. All he saw was her.

He wanted to take things slowly, but knew it was impossible; what his body and all his screaming senses demanded was an imperative mating, a fusing of two bodies in heated necessity, and that compulsive need was almost beyond even his powerful will to control. All he could do was struggle not to give in completely to the wildness of it.

Wolfe kissed her again hungrily, his mouth slanting across hers to deepen the contact, and her passionate response made his body tremble. He felt her fingers pulling at the buttons of his shirt, and helped her by shrugging it off when she pushed the material over his shoulders. Then she was touching him, her fingers gliding over his chest as if she wanted to learn him by touch alone.

Her slender fingers probed through the thick mat of hair to the hard flesh beneath, exploring. She found and touched his nipples, rubbing the tight little buds slowly with just the tips of her fingers, and he shuddered again at the hot wave of pleasure washing over him.

When he lifted his head, making another vain attempt to control his breathing, she was looking up at him with darkened, gleaming eyes. "You feel good," she whispered, her fingers still probing and gently caressing him.

He was almost mesmerized by the absorbed, wondering expression on her small face, and more than seduced by her hands on him. He wanted to tell her how wonderful she felt to him, how touching her caused the hot blood of need to roar in his veins and being touched by her brought a pleasure almost too great to bear. But he couldn't say anything.

He couldn't respond to her the way he had responded to other women when desire had gripped him, with seductive words to match his caresses and casual compliments that were more appreciation of beauty than an aspect of intimacy. The words and phrases of an easygoing lover that had always come so effortlessly to him were out of his reach now.

Never a silent lover, he became more of one with her, because what he felt was something too profound for practiced lovemaking, something too ancient to have words.

Wolfe made a rough sound, almost a growl, and swiftly pulled her top off over her head. Storm caught her breath at the abrupt action, but willingly lifted her arms and pulled them free of the garment. They were so close that her naked breasts brushed against his chest, and both of them sucked in a breath at the contact.

Storm stared up at him, feeling his hands on her shoulders slowly drawing her toward him until her tightening nipples nestled in the thick mat of hair covering his hard chest. It obviously felt as good to him as it did to her, because his heavy-lidded eyes burned with pleasure and the curve of his mouth was incredibly sensual, and she felt an intense satisfaction at the knowledge that he found her exciting.

Her hands slid over his hard ribs and then around his waist to his back, fingers probing the smoothness of his skin and the power of his taut muscles. She could barely breathe, and the unfamiliar restless feeling of a hot, growing tension was gripping her body like a fever. All the strength seemed to seep from her legs, so that she leaned into him, and a little whimper escaped her when her breasts pressed fully against his chest.

Wolfe's arms went around her, one hand tangled in her thick hair and the other sliding down her back to press her lower body strongly against his. She could feel a tremor in him, like something stretched too tightly, and it was in his low, hoarse voice when he said, "Easy."

As inexperienced as Storm was, some part of her understood what he was saying. She understood that what was between them was so powerful and primitive it could hardly be controlled—and that he was trying to control it.

"No," she whispered, rising on her tiptoes against him as her arms went up around his neck. "It can't be easy . . . don't you know? Can't you feel it?"

He was still for an instant, almost frozen, as if he was denying her certainty. But then he made a rough sound and bent his head to kiss her, his mouth so hungry it made her ache to give him everything she was. She felt him move, heard the whisper of the bedcovers being pulled back, and then he lifted her and placed her in the middle of the bed.

Storm was so dizzy she didn't open her eyes right away because she was afraid the room would be spinning, but when she felt his hands at her hips, she had to look at him. His handsome face was hard, intent, molded by desire into a stark mask of ancient male sensuality, his eyes burning. She had never known a man could look like that, never known how beautiful and primitive a man's passion could be.

It stole her breath and her will and all her strength, leaving her nothing except the burning hunger he had created in her and the instincts born in the caves.

He stripped the tight leggings off her in one smooth motion, getting rid of the socks as well, and she was vaguely astonished to find herself lying naked. But the way he was looking at her made her forget everything except the vast, overwhelming, compelling need to belong to him. Nothing else seemed to matter very much.

She heard a couple of thuds as his shoes hit the floor, and then Wolfe was beside her on the bed. He was still wearing his pants, and she had the dim understanding that it was because he was still trying not to lose control, but before she could react to that, she felt the incredibly erotic shock of his mouth on her breast.

She felt her body arch as a soft cry of surprise and pleasure escaped her, and her hands clutched at his shoulders convulsively. She couldn't believe how he was making her feel, how it was possible to feel these amazing sensations. His big hand surrounded one breast, kneading gently, his thumb brushing over the tightly beaded point, while his mouth held the other throbbing nipple in a shattering caress.

Storm slid her shaking fingers into his thick hair and held his head, only dimly aware of a whimper that seemed to come from someplace so deep inside her she hadn't even known it was there. Pleasure washed over her in burning waves, each one stronger than the last, and her body took on a separate life, a consciousness of its own beyond her control. She couldn't be still, couldn't slow the pounding of her heart or stop the unfamiliar little sounds of need.

Then she felt his hand slip lower, touching her, and the burst of raw sensation was so acute it was almost pain. Exquisite pain. He was stroking her damp, swollen flesh very gently in a stunning, heart-stopping rhythm her body craved, and she was instantly swept up in the mindless, primitive drive toward release.

Storm writhed as the tension built toward a peak, pressing the back of her hand to her mouth to muffle the sounds she could feel rising inside her. Wolfe pushed her hand away and covered her mouth with his, still caressing her insistently, and she moaned wordlessly.

For an eternal instant she wanted to fight him as well as her own body, panicked by the sheer power of the feelings sweeping over her, but instinct took over and she let go as the tension finally shattered. Her entire body convulsed, shuddering as unbelievable ecstasy gripped her in pulsing waves, and she cried out wildly. It seemed to last forever, burning and throbbing while her body shivered under the impact of it, until finally the pleasure ebbed gently away and Storm went limp, almost sobbing.

Six

Wolfe held her for a moment longer, pressing kisses to her flushed face, and then he quickly rolled off the bed. Storm was still trying to catch her breath, overwhelmed by what had just happened to her, and wasn't completely aware of what he was doing until he returned to her.

When she felt the bed move and realized he was with her again, she also realized that he was naked and that he had assumed responsibility for their lovemaking. It didn't surprise her, because she had been sure he was both careful and responsible, and it made her feel her trust in him had not been misplaced.

She returned to his arms eagerly, sharp excitement building in her again. The fierce heat in his eyes seduced her as surely as his hands and mouth had taught her the meaning of ecstasy, and there was nothing on earth she wanted more than to please him. But despite the strain she could see in his taut face and feel in the trembling, rigid muscles of his powerful body, it soon became obvious that Wolfe was still holding on to the last few threads of his control.

He was caressing her again, his hands stroking her body as if the feeling of her skin was something he craved. He kissed her, the deep, hungry kisses that had the power to set her on fire, then trailed his lips down over her throat. Storm closed her eyes, her hands sliding over the sleek, damp flesh of his back and shoulders, her breathing growing quick and shallow as his mouth moved with agonizing slowness toward an aching nipple.

Wolfe didn't know how much longer he could hold back, but his patience and struggle were being rewarded by the sweetest torment he'd ever known. In delaying a completion every fiber in his body cried out for, he found himself so sensitized that the lightest brush of her fingertips and the heat of her skin under his own touch made him quiver from the bones out.

There was an intense focusing of all his senses, as if nothing in the world existed except her. Her gleaming emerald eyes. The soft, reddened lips, so erotic they beckoned him irresistibly. Her round breasts, fitting his hands as if designed only for him, flushed and swollen, the velvety nipples so sensitive they seemed to pulse in his mouth. Her passion-heated skin, as smooth as silk, unbelievably soft. The supple strength of her slender, delicate body. The uncontrolled little sounds she made in passion.

Wolfe wanted to make it last forever, hungry for more of this unfamiliar, all-consuming obsession, but his body ached intolerably and he knew he'd explode or go completely out of his mind if he delayed much longer.

She was ready for him, her desire peaking a second time under the onslaught of his hands and mouth. Her tense, trembling body was caught up in the drive for release, and he couldn't hold back any longer. He eased her legs apart and moved between them, rising above her as her hands lifted to his shoulders.

Their eyes locked together, blue fire and emerald softness, and her lips parted with a quick, indrawn breath when she felt the blunt pressure of his body seeking entrance. And perhaps it was because she had waited so long that giving herself to a man for the first time had such a profound effect on her . . . or perhaps it was simply because she was giving herself in love.

She couldn't believe the sensations, the stark intimacy. She could feel her flesh stretching, feel the resistance of her body. There was an enormous pressure, an overwhelming sense of being invaded by an irresistible force beyond her control. For an instant she felt panic, a female's instinctive fear of vulnerability, but then he whispered her name, his voice all but gone, and the anxiety faded. She could never match his strength, but she trusted him not to use it against her.

She stared up at his face, so hard and handsome, into the blazing eyes that made her think of eagles, and her arms slid around his neck. The burning pressure was increasing, edging into pain, but even then she didn't want him to stop. She wanted to belong to him, and she knew he was being as careful as he could. The desire he had created in her was still there, hovering, and because he had thoroughly satisfied her once before, her body's reluctance to admit him was less than it might have been, but he was a big man and she didn't accept him easily.

She cried out without meaning to when something gave way inside her with a sudden sharp pain, surprised when the pain immediately began to ebb. Wolfe made a low, rough sound as his body settled gently into the cradle of hers, his face tightening in a spasm of fierce pleasure.

Storm was just a little tense for a moment or two, her senses and attention turned inward as she felt herself adjust to all the alien sensations of his possession. She was both relieved and delighted when she realized that with the stubborn barrier gone, their bodies seemed to fit together perfectly.

There was no pain now, and the pressure was more a sense of profound closeness.

When he lowered his head and kissed her, she responded instantly, wildly, the hovering desire sweeping over her once more. Her hands stroked over his back and shoulders, and she loved the feeling of her breasts pressed to his chest, his hard belly against hers, his weight on her.

Wolfe watched her face, holding on to the last whisper of his control as he began to move carefully. He slipped his forearms underneath her shoulders to hold her even closer, his fingers sliding into her thick hair. She made a little sound and raised her head far enough to kiss him, her green eyes gleaming at him, and her hips lifted instinctively in a sensual feminine answer to his slow thrusts.

Her enticing movements beneath him yanked a groan from Wolfe, driving his desire for her impossibly higher. She was so tight around him, so silky, her body clasping his in a soft, heated grasp like nothing he'd ever felt before. He tried to hold back, tried to be careful, but her fervent response defeated his will. She was as fearless in passion as she was in anger.

He thought it was a kind of madness, when he could think, later, but whatever it was, it was beyond pleasure. It was a mutual possession, a joining too intense to be anything except a kind of bonding.

It swept them both along on a surging tide, and this time Storm let it take her without a struggle. The tension wound tighter and tighter, making her writhe and moan, making pleading sounds she didn't recognize come from her throat. When she didn't think she could bear it another second, the awful tension snapped, and everything inside her seemed to turn into liquid, pulsing heat.

The internal shudders of her pleasure caught Wolfe, caressing him, and the exploding force of his own release washed over him in a tide of pure sensation. It ripped a guttural cry from somewhere deep in his chest, and drained him so utterly that he had no strength left even to wonder what had happened to him.

Wolfe didn't remember much of the next minutes. He thought they both dozed for a little while, still lying close together on the tumbled bed. He knew he didn't let go of her even in sleep, both his arms wrapped around her as if he thought someone might try to take her away from him.

That was unusual for him, and a bit unnerving.

It occurred to him that it was probably still early. He couldn't see his watch since his arm was covered by the warm weight of her hair, so he turned his head far enough to see the clock on the nightstand. It told him it wasn't yet eight o'clock in the evening.

Storm lifted her head from his shoulder then, startling him; he hadn't realized she was awake. And if he'd tried to predict her first words after having taken a man to her bed for the first time, he would have missed by a mile. As usual, her reaction was completely unexpected.

Her green eyes were grave and her lazy voice unutterably sweet when she said, "Thank you."

Wolfe felt something inside him turn over with a peculiar, almost painful lurch. "For what?" he murmured, lifting one hand to brush back baby-fine strands of her golden hair. His fingers lingered to stroke her warm, silky skin.

She smiled. "For being my first lover. You made it wonderful for me."

"I hurt you," he said.

Storm was matter-of-fact. "I expected that. But it wasn't bad at all, because you made me want you so much I barely felt the pain. I know it could have been a lot worse. I don't think it was easy for you, having to be so patient with me, and I just want you to know I'm grateful."

There was nothing in her green eyes except honesty, and Wolfe felt another of those odd little lurches inside him. He'd never before been thanked for making love to a woman, and didn't really know how to respond. Especially since he thought it would have taken an absolute monster to *not* be careful with her, given her delicacy and her virginity. He didn't know whether to point out that fact to her, or simply accept her thanks with what grace he could muster.

Finally opting for the latter because he needed to try to keep things casual between them, he said a bit dryly, "Don't mention it."

Storm smiled at him and kissed his chin, then pushed herself up onto an elbow. "I'm probably being hideously unromantic in thinking of food at a time like this," she said, "but it's nearly eight and lunch was a long time ago. Why don't we order something from room service?"

"We can go out if you'd rather," he told her.

"I'd rather stay here with you." Then she hesitated, and there was a flash of vulnerability in her eyes, gone so quickly he almost didn't recognize it. Her voice remained casual and matter-of-fact when she asked, "You are planning to stay the night, aren't you?"

His hand had fallen to her shoulder when she moved, and his long fingers probed the fineness of small bones under silky skin. He wasn't surprised at the roughening sound of his own voice when he muttered, "If I'm invited, I plan to stay here all weekend. We'll discuss next week later."

Storm said merely, "You're invited," and tilted her head briefly to rub her cheek against his hand. Then she pulled gently away from him and slid from the bed.

Naked, she was sexy in a way he'd never known a woman to be, her wild hair flowing over her shoulders to veil her breasts, her petite body perfectly formed. He couldn't take his eyes off her. But he saw her wince slightly as she got to her feet, and concern for her tempered his renewing desire. "If you take a warm bath now, your muscles will appreciate it later," he said lightly.

She stretched cautiously, entirely unselfconscious, and made a slight face. "I think you may be right. I'm not used to doing anything in bed except sleeping or reading a book."

Telling himself there would be plenty of time to satisfy this hunger he felt for her, Wolfe sat up and swung his feet to the floor. Light. He needed to keep things light and casual. "I'll get the menu and place the order. By the time you finish your bath, the food should be here."

"Sounds like a plan." She smiled at him and went into the bathroom, and a moment later he heard the tub beginning to fill.

He got out of bed and found his briefs and pants, but didn't bother with his shirt except to pick it and Storm's things up off the floor and toss the clothing over a chair. He went into the living room of the suite to find the room-service menu, and it wasn't until he got the folder from the top of the television that he remembered the third occupant of the suite.

Bear was exactly where he had been all along, on the back of the couch near Wolfe's black leather jacket, sort of crouched in that odd position cats seemed to find comfortable—his paws folded under him and his long tail tucked alongside him. He regarded Wolfe enigmatically through green eyes eerily like Storm's.

"Hello," Wolfe said experimentally. He was unaccustomed to cats, but had the feeling he should speak to this one.

Either Bear was feeling unsocial, or simply hadn't decided whether to accept a man's—or this man's—presence in Storm's life, because he remained silent. And that vivid little face with its clear green eyes remained enigmatic.

"So much for that," Wolfe muttered, and carried the room-service menu back into the bedroom. He glanced at the menu, realized he didn't have the faintest idea what Storm might like for her supper, and went to the bathroom door. It was open a few inches, and the water was still running in the tub. He knocked lightly on the door and asked if she was decent.

Storm sounded amused. "No, but come in anyway." When he obeyed, she said, "Could you turn the water off, please? I don't want to move."

He did as she asked, his attention once more completely taken up by her; it was as if his awareness of her was so powerful there was no room left in him for anything else. She was lying back in the large oval tub, up to her neck in bubbles. Her hair was piled somewhat carelessly atop her head, which made her appear even more delicate and, to Wolfe, wildly sexy in yet another way. He couldn't stop staring at her. And between the steamy heat of the small room and the haunting scent of the bubble bath—the exotic fragrance he associated only with her—he was having a hard time thinking about anything except her.

"Thank you," she murmured, her head resting back on the lip of the tub. She looked up at him with slumberous eyes, and a contented smile curved her lips. "You ought to get a medal for suggesting this."

"I'll think up a reward for later," he said, going down on one knee on the mat beside the tub. He forced himself to concentrate on practicalities. "In the meantime what do you want from room service?"

He opened the menu and held it above the bubbles so she could see it.

Storm sighed luxuriously. "I could get used to this."

Before Wolfe could frame a retort, the phone in the bedroom shrilled a summons. Storm shook the bubbles off her hands and took the menu away from him, saying she still wasn't ready to move, so he went out to answer the phone.

Whoever it was obviously didn't want to talk to him, hanging up after an instant of silence. When he returned to the bathroom, Wolfe said ominously, "If a man answers . . ."

Undisturbed, she said promptly, "Yeah, except you're on the wrong end of that equation. I'd only tell a lover to hang up if I was married and afraid my husband would answer. It was obviously just a wrong number. Does chicken sound good to you? Or are you a steak-and-potatoes man?"

"I'm a food man, not at all picky."

"Glad to hear it." Storm handed the menu back to him and pointed out exactly what she wanted, then told him to order whatever he liked for himself. "I'm on an expense account, and Ace is paying," she said.

Wolfe lifted an eyebrow at her. "Is that usual?"

"For me it is. One of the perks for being willing to go wherever they send me." She eyed him with amusement. "And even if they found out they were feeding you this weekend, they wouldn't object. As I understand it, when you threw your weight around, and added Max Bannister's in for good measure, my boss was willing to do just about anything to please you. In case you're interested, it cost them big bucks to pull me off the job in Paris and get me here fast enough to suit you."

Wolfe smiled wryly. "Shows you what can be accomplished by a bit of fire and brimstone and a dash or two of blackmail."

She chuckled and then closed her eyes. "I have a feeling you're pretty good at that sort of thing. I certainly *know* about your ability to conjure the fire and brimstone."

"Look who's talking. Do you want coffee, tea, or a soft drink?"

"No—milk. I'll need my strength."

Wolfe decided not to comment on that, and left the bathroom to place their order with room service. He wanted to go back to her afterward, to offer to wash her back so he could touch her again, but he resisted the urge.

She seemed utterly comfortable with him, unselfconscious and casual, but having a lover was new to Storm and he didn't want to overwhelm her with his growing need to be close to her, to touch her constantly. Especially since he had so stubbornly resisted being her lover in the first place.

Lover. That was it, Wolfe thought as he waited restlessly for her to finish her bath, that was what was different. He had been a lover in a technical sense, but this was the first time he had *felt* like one. Always before, it had been a matter of sex, of satisfying physical desires—and once sated, those desires had vanished.

He had always preferred to be in someone else's bed, because then he could leave with little fuss; a woman in his bed was a rare occurrence, and one that had made him uncomfortable. He'd never felt a need to remain with a woman after sex, had never craved closeness or simple physical contact.

With Storm he did. He kept remembering how her skin felt under his touch, how soft her lips were, how her pale hair felt like spun silk, the weight of her breast in his hand and the taste of her nipple in his mouth; it was as if the memory of those erotic textures lingered on his fingertips and his mouth, living images that were now a part of him. As if she were imprinted on his senses.

It should have disturbed him, that realization, because he had never let anyone get that close, but instead what he felt was a deep, almost fierce elation. He didn't examine the emotion or question it in any way, he just accepted it. Like being Storm's lover, it was something he found unexpectedly exhilarating.

Room service delivered their meal about ten minutes later, and the waiter had just left when Storm came into the living room. She was wearing a short, silky nightgown in a pale pink with a print negligee open over it, and with her feet bare and her hair still piled high on her head she was so beautiful it almost stopped his heart.

Though he wanted to keep things casual, he couldn't resist touching her. So when she reached him, he did, one hand at her tiny waist and the other cupping her face as he pushed her chin up gently and fitted his mouth to hers. He couldn't make it a casual kiss, because his hunger for her was too intense, but he did manage not to fling her over his shoulder and carry her back to the bedroom.

Storm responded instantly and sweetly, her hands lifting to rest on his chest, her soft mouth alive beneath his, and when he at last raised his head, she smiled up at him with unshadowed pleasure. "You do that very well," she murmured. "But I suppose you know that. With all your experience, I mean."

Since he was beginning to anticipate her singular honesty, the comment didn't unnerve him—but he could feel a wry smile tugging at his lips. "Has it occurred to you that it could have absolutely nothing to do with experience, and everything to do with a certain . . . chemical reaction between two people?"

Still smiling, Storm moved away from him toward the dining table past the couch where the waiter had placed their food. "Chemical reaction?"

He thought that despite her smile his question bothered her, but he wasn't sure. Still, Wolfe wished he could have taken back the words. He had only intended to steer the conversation away from any discussion about his past sexual experience, not to sound so dispassionate about it. Before he could try to clarify what he'd meant, Storm spoke again.

"Is that a common thing? Chemical reactions?" She sat down at the table and began unfolding her napkin, looking across at him with simple curiosity. "I mean, if you watch TV or go to the movies, you see some pretty intense passion that rarely lasts for long. Do the chemicals lose their potency, or what?"

"Why ask me?" He went to his own place at the table and sat down.

"I thought you'd know if anybody would."

He looked for signs of sarcasm or mockery in her expressive face and honest eyes, and found none. Her seriousness disturbed him, because he was torn between the urge to assure her that she was—that *they* were—special, and the wariness he still felt about committing himself.

Finally he said, "I believe you once pointed out to me that I must be satisfied with brief, surface relationships—given my track record. So I'm probably the wrong person to ask about lasting passions." He didn't like that response any more than he had his earlier one, but he was finding it impossible to talk to her about this.

Storm nodded gravely. "I hadn't thought about it that way, but I suppose you're right." With a slight shrug she abandoned the subject. "Listen, I've always wanted to see a ball game in Candlestick Park, and the Giants are home this weekend. How does that sound for tomorrow night?"

Wolfe agreed that it sounded like fun, relieved by the change of subject, and during the next few minutes he found himself engaged in a spirited debate with Storm about the pennant chances of various baseball teams. It didn't really surprise him that she was as knowledgeable about the sport as she seemed to be about everything else that interested her, especially when she ruefully pointed out that as one of only two females in a family containing seven males, learning to appreciate sports had been a simple matter of self-preservation.

By the time their meal was finished, Wolfe discovered that she was not only a baseball fan but also enjoyed football and hockey, despised basketball and boxing, was bored by tennis except as a player, and became unashamedly sentimental and patriotic during Olympic competition.

She had strong and definite views about politics and world affairs but was nonetheless able to discuss both without losing her temper, and it didn't appear to disturb her in the slightest whenever Wolfe disagreed with her.

By the time room service had cleared away the clutter left from their meal, and they were sitting together on the couch, he realized without much surprise that he was even more fascinated by her. No matter what they talked about, he found himself listening to her with utter absorption and watching her expressive face with pure enjoyment. He was so wrapped up in her that he felt an unfamiliar sense of vulnerability, an odd, achingly disturbing worry that—committed or not—what he felt for this woman was more intense than whatever she felt for him.

Because he didn't know what she felt for him. Desire, yes; she had made that plain from the beginning. But she seemed to view that desire with a lightness and nonchalance he had to struggle very hard to match.

If she was aware of the effect she had on him, Storm didn't show it. She was so relaxed and comfortable with him that it seemed obvious she considered this new stage in their relationship what she had professed she could "handle"—a casual affair that would last no more than a few weeks.

But, true to her word, she didn't bring up their relationship in any way. It was clear that as far as she was concerned, Wolfe had tacitly accepted her terms when he had taken the step to meet her halfway, and that was all the assurance she needed.

Wolfe was fully aware of the irony of this. He had fought stubbornly against giving in to her, and yet now it was he who needed some kind of reassurance, some sign or word from her that would let him know *she* felt more than mere desire. The problem was, since it was not something he'd ever needed before, he didn't know how to ask. And he didn't know if he even had the right to ask after his reluctance to provide her with any assurances.

"You've gone all quiet."

Wolfe turned his head and looked at her. She was on her knees beside him on the couch, turned toward him. She had been petting Bear, but the little cat had gotten down off the couch and gone to curl up on a chair by the window—which sort of relieved Wolfe; he didn't think that cat liked him very much.

"Have I?" He smiled at her. "I'm sorry."

Storm shook her head slightly. "No reason to be sorry. But if there's something you want to talk about . . . ?"

He hesitated, but finally shook his head. His feelings were too new and too unfamiliar for him to be ready to examine them closely. "No, not really." He gestured slightly toward the coffee table, where Storm's notes, diagrams, and other paperwork were piled high. "You brought a lot of work home."

Gravely Storm said, "Well, having bragged I could get the new system written and on-line in ten days or less, I've had to work pretty hard. It's my own fault, though."

Wolfe didn't disagree with that, but he did frown. "I won't hold you to that estimate. If you can get the system on-line anytime in the next two weeks or so, we'll still be ahead of our original schedule."

"Good, then I'll take the weekend off," she said promptly. Her hands lifted to his shoulders, her fingers probing the hardness of muscle and bone. "If I get a better offer, that is."

His hands found her tiny waist, and as always, once he touched her he couldn't think about anything else. "What would you consider a better offer?" he murmured, slowly drawing her toward him.

Just before her lips met his, Storm whispered, "Whatever you've got in mind."

Earlier, Wolfe had contained his hunger for her by reminding himself that this was new to her, that she would need time—physically if not emotionally—to adjust to having a lover. But Storm made it plain that she wasn't in the least uncomfortable in any way, and that she had no intention of taking things easy or allowing him to hold back for her sake.

She was astonishingly passionate, uninhibited and generous, and when Wolfe carried her to their bed, he was far beyond the ability to hold back any part of himself.

It was long after midnight when the lamplit room became peaceful again and Storm fell asleep in his arms. As before, Wolfe thought he might have dozed, but not for long. He found himself awake, listening to her breathing and feeling it warm against his skin. Careful not to wake her, he stroked her wonderful hair, her back, shaped the curve of her hip as she lay against him.

He couldn't resist touching her, and he'd more or less stopped trying. He had also stopped trying to convince himself that his obsession with her was something that would burn white-hot only for a while before dying down to ashes. The truth was, this slight, drawling, green-eyed woman with her erotic mouth and fearless temper had touched something in him that had never been touched before. He hadn't meant to let her get under his skin, but she'd gotten there somehow. He'd been right in thinking she was a woman who would carve her mark on a man's life.

On his heart.

Storm stirred when she felt the bed move and the warmth of his body leave her. She opened one eye, saw the sun shining through the drapes, and immediately closed it again. "Oh, God, it's the crack of dawn," she murmured.

Wolfe bent back over the bed and kissed her cheek, then her mouth when she turned her head toward him. "It's not that early," he told her. "Almost eight. I'm going to take a shower."

She turned over onto her stomach and half buried her face in the pillow, and let out a muffled groan. "I need more sleep." She heard him chuckle, thought that his morning voice was slightly raspy and very sexy, and kept her eyes closed until she heard the shower begin running.

It was difficult for her to think so early in the morning, and there was a large part of her that simply wanted to enjoy what she had found with Wolfe, but as always, her sense of responsibility nagged at her. She raised herself up on her elbows and looked toward the bathroom door, where steam wafted out from his shower, and her sigh was a bit ragged.

After a moment she pulled herself to the edge of the bed and sat up. She reached for the phone and called a familiar number and, when he answered, said, "Don't call here again; he'd notice another wrong number. I'll have to keep in touch with you."

A bit grimly he said, "Do you know what you're doing?"

Storm let out the ghost of a laugh. "I've been asking myself that for days. But . . . it's a little late to turn back now."

He was silent for a moment, and when he spoke again, his cool voice held a note of genuine concern. "What are you going to do when he finds out the truth? I know him, Storm, and I can tell you that to him, a betrayal of trust is worse than anything else could be. He won't forgive easily. Maybe not at all."

She continued to gaze blindly toward the bathroom door. "I know. But like I said . . . it's a little late to turn back. You said once that I didn't have a choice. I still don't." She drew a quick breath. "I'll probably be with him most of the day, and maybe tomorrow too, so it's best if I call you from the museum on Monday."

"Take care," he said quietly.

Storm cradled the receiver and sat there on the edge of the bed for a moment, an aching inside her that might have been her heart. It had taken all her resolution not to tell Wolfe that she loved him; only the knowledge that she couldn't tell him that when so much else was lies had kept her silent.

The worst lie was the one he would see when he finally discovered the truth. He would realize that part of her job had been to distract him, to keep his attention away from the installation of the new computer program and his suspicions away from Ace Security for as long as possible. He would see that very clearly. And he would very likely believe that her determined pursuit of him had been a means to that end.

Storm didn't know if he would ever believe her when she denied that, but she didn't have very much hope. If he knew her well enough . . . perhaps. If he cared about her enough to forgive the betrayal of trust . . . perhaps. If he understood her reasons . . . perhaps.

All she knew for certain was that her time with Wolfe was precious. And all she could do was make the most of that time, gather all the experiences and memories of them together to hoard against the prospect of what could come.

Without thinking about it very much, Storm rose from the bed and went to the bathroom. She pushed the door open and looked through the steamy room toward the shower stall. She could see his powerful, imposing form through the frosted glass, and her mouth went a little dry as she watched him move.

It was so hard to act casual when all her senses went crazy if she just looked at him. So hard to pretend her heart didn't beat faster if he was near, that her very bones didn't melt when he touched her. And it was a whisper away from impossible to lie beneath him in bed, going out of her mind with pleasure, and not cry out the stark truth that she loved him.

Storm took the few steps necessary to cross the bathroom and open the door of the shower stall. She slipped in with him. He must have seen through the door that she'd been watching him, because he wasn't surprised. He pulled her immediately into his arms, his eyes glittering with hunger, his hard mouth finding her soft one, and she was dimly glad that the spray of the shower hid from him the existence of her tears.

Seven

Morgan West had found the last week more than a little challenging. Since the museum's curator, Kenneth Dugan, had been occupied by a series of fund-raisers, she had offered to take care of most of his duties—her own duties as the director of the *Mysteries Past* exhibit being very light at the moment—and found herself stuck in her office most of the time either dealing with paperwork or else on the phone.

She had managed to spend a little time with Storm Tremaine, finding the petite blonde to be good company and very much enjoying observing the romantic struggle between Storm and Wolfe. It was her private opinion that Wolfe—like his namesake in that painting on the museum's second floor—was on the verge of being blindsided by a bolt of lightning, and she'd decided that it couldn't have happened to a more deserving man.

So that was very interesting to watch, and she looked forward to seeing more.

But there was something else that had been occupying much of her thoughts and what time she could spare. It was a small matter of the thief she had been unwillingly charmed by in the witching hours of a dark night—and the necklace he had stolen right off her neck.

Morgan had told herself at least a hundred times that there was nothing she could do to get her necklace back. Max had told her, with his usual courtesy but with emphasis, that there were enough people after Quinn's hide without her involvement.

Well, she knew that.

But. She wanted her necklace back. Max had tried, but if Quinn had sold the thing—the only reason she could think of for him to have taken it other than sheer deviltry, which was admittedly just as likely—it had yet to surface anywhere. She wanted it back.

That was why, she told herself. That was why she was sticking her nose in despite Max's warning and her own common sense. Because she wanted her necklace back. *Not* because she had any desire at all to meet up with that devious thief again.

He was still in the city, she knew that. She could feel him, like an itch at the back of her neck, and had the unnerving belief that at least twice he had actually been in the museum, lost among the crowd of visitors, and close enough to touch. She had no idea what his face looked like, and though she caught herself studying several tall strangers with an intentness that had resulted in two indecent propositions and three requests for a date, she was reasonably sure she hadn't actually seen him.

But ever since her last encounter with him, she'd been looking for him. And not just in the museum where she worked. She spent, on the average, at least a couple of hours every night in her car, parked outside some other museum or jewelry store—any likely target—waiting to see if he would show up. It was dumb and reckless and she knew it . . . but she couldn't help herself.

On this particular Saturday night, however, Morgan had more or less convinced herself that she was wasting her time. Quinn was the most infamous cat burglar in the world, for God's sake, and most of the police forces in existence had been after him for at least ten years. There was just no way her amateur efforts were going to locate him.

She found that thought depressing.

Since she had no other plans for the evening and was feeling too restless to sit at home and read or watch television, Morgan decided around eight that night to go to the museum and pick up some paperwork she could deal with over the weekend. It wasn't unusual for her to go to the museum after hours, and one of the guards let her in as soon as he saw her from inside the lobby.

"Hi, Steve," she said cheerfully as she came in. "Anything happening today?"

The middle-aged guard shook his head. "Nah, not much. Mr. Dugan was here most of the day. Oh—and Mr. Bannister's back in the city. He dropped by a few minutes ago to take a look at the *Mysteries Past* wing. Had somebody with him. A cop, I think."

Morgan frowned at him. "A cop? Are you sure?"

"Well, he was wearing a gun in a shoulder holster, that much I'm sure of. I guess he could have been some kind of bodyguard for Mr. Bannister, but he didn't act that way. Hold on a second." The guard went to the desk in one corner of the lobby, spoke with a second guard seated there, and studied the logbook briefly. Then he returned to Morgan. "Mr. Bannister signed them in—himself and a guest, unnamed. They're still here, according to Brian. Upstairs at the exhibit, most likely. I'll sign you in, Morgan."

She nodded her thanks a bit absently and, instead of moving toward the hallway of offices on the first floor, chose instead to head for the stairs, and the west wing of the second floor. She was surprised that Max was back from his honeymoon weeks earlier than expected, but even more, she was curious to see who he had brought to inspect the exhibit wing.

She was casually dressed in jeans and a sweater, her long hair in a neat ponytail, and her sneakers made no sound on the marble floor as Morgan moved swiftly up the stairs. She didn't have to worry about using her keycard to deactivate corridor alarms or other security devices, since those in this wing were currently inactive; nothing of value was in place yet, so there was nothing to protect.

Morgan wasn't sneaky about it, but as she began making her way through the wing she found herself walking with lighter steps and being cautious. After all, she told herself, since Max had brought this man here after hours and hadn't recorded his name in the security logbook, perhaps no one was meant to know—officially, anyway—about his presence.

Of course, that did nothing to deter Morgan. She was nothing if not curious.

Moving as silently as a whisper, she paused finally in the shadow of a darkened display case quite a bit larger than she was, where she had a perfect view of the two men. They were standing some yards away, in the main room of the exhibit, where other display cases were lighted as if for inspection. But neither man was looking at the cases.

In fact, Max was leaning back against one of them carelessly, and the other man was drumming his long fingers against glass that would, when the collection was in place, bristle with touch-sensitive alarms.

The two men were a striking pair. Both wore dark raincoats, and there was a curious similarity in them that had little to do with physical appearance and much more to do with stance and a kind of inner toughness that was visible in both. The man who was a stranger to Morgan was slightly over six feet tall and built athletically, with gleaming sable hair and odd, light-colored eyes that looked sharp enough to cut;

he was handsome in a strikingly elegant way, almost aristocratic and curiously foreign. Max was a couple of inches taller, broader through the shoulders and visibly more powerful in terms of physical strength; his black hair, steel-gray eyes, and rugged good looks would have tagged him as an American in any city of the world.

Morgan didn't move and hardly breathed, watching them intently and listening as they talked; she only wished she'd been privy to the beginning of the conversation.

"Second thoughts?" the stranger asked Max.

"You know better than that, Jared. I gave my word, and I mean to keep it. The collection will be displayed here, as planned." As usual, Max's voice was low and calm, and unexpectedly soft for a man who looked as if he'd been hewn from granite.

"No matter what?" Jared's handsome face held a somewhat wry expression as he looked at the other man.

"Nothing's changed. Your people at Interpol have tried for years, like police all over the world, but nobody's even gotten close. You have to have bait for a trap, and the only bait with any chance of catching him is the Bannister collection."

Jared expelled breath in a rough sigh. "That sounds so simple, dammit. Why am I having nightmares?"

"Because you're a sensitive soul?" Max murmured.

Jared said something rude, then sighed again. "Look, I'm sorry I called you back early, but we have a number of problems. The biggest one looming right in front of us is your security expert."

Max cleared his throat. "Well, it's not as if we didn't expect as much."

"That doesn't alter the fact that he's going to raise hell and breathe fire when he finds out what we're planning to do. Tell me something. Did we ever have a plan for that eventuality?"

124 • KAY HOOPER

Rubbing the back of his neck with one hand, Max said ruefully, "As I recall, we decided to jump off that bridge when we came to it."

"That's how I remembered it. Damn."

"Well, we can—" Max broke off abruptly, turning his head to look toward the doorway. Morgan froze, but she had the weird feeling he saw her.

"What?" Jared asked, tensing visibly.

Max looked back at him, calm as always. "Nothing. But maybe we'd better finish this discussion somewhere else."

Morgan didn't wait to hear any more. Moving as swiftly and silently as she could, she slipped away and hurried down the stairs to the first-floor lobby. She went to her office and picked up the papers she'd wanted, hoping that if Max came down before she got out, he'd see her homework and not ask questions.

But he wasn't in the lobby when she signed out at the desk, or when Steve reappeared to see her out of the museum. Morgan thought she was probably as casual and cheerful with the guard as always, but since her thoughts were in a whirl, she couldn't be sure of anything.

She got into her small car and immediately pulled away from the curb in front of the museum, but she drove only a couple of blocks before she pulled over and turned off the engine. She was halfway home, only two blocks from her apartment building, but she had no interest in going home.

Her first coherent thought was, characteristically, a spurt of annoyance at Max. He might have told her, she fumed silently. Then she wondered if he *would* have told her—if she hadn't encountered Quinn. And if that encounter hadn't affected her more than she wanted to admit. Max was perceptive; he probably knew she'd been unwillingly charmed by Quinn.

Because that had to be it. Max was working with a man from Interpol, allowing his priceless collection to be bait for a trap set to catch Quinn.

Morgan didn't know quite how she felt about that, and not knowing unnerved her. She should have been cheering, she told herself grimly. One less thief in the world was, after all, a thing to cheer for. And even though Quinn's reputation described him as two parts ghost and one part shadow, Morgan had felt the reality of him; he was a man, and men could be caught if the trap was good enough.

After a few moments she started her car again and pulled away from the curb. But she didn't go to her apartment. Instead she went across town to the museum that was next on her mental list of places Quinn might find inviting. She cussed at herself for doing it, but even her own scornful words failed to have much effect on her. Sighing, she stopped for coffee in a paper cup and parked on a street with a view of the rear of the museum, locked her car doors, and settled down to wait.

Sipping her coffee and watching the big building that was shrouded by an incoming fog, Morgan slumped down in her seat and brooded about Quinn. Would the trap being set by Max and the man from Interpol catch Quinn? Could it? Quinn had built a reputation for being daring, nerveless—and utterly scornful of so-called security. In fact, he seemed to delight in flaunting his seeming wizardry in slipping undetected through the electronic mazes of state-of-the-art technology.

Would the security system Storm was busy creating pose any more of a problem for Quinn than all those he had so effortlessly flaunted? No, Morgan realized slowly, there had to be more to it than that. If a *trap* was being set, then there had to be a deliberate weakness somewhere, a hole—or at least a soft spot—where a thief could see it and believe it was there by accident. He would have to be guided into place, lured into a position where he could be caught.

Morgan continued to brood about that for nearly two hours, long after she'd finished her cold coffee. Finally she told herself she was being an idiot and sat up. This was ridiculous! She hadn't a hope in hell of finding Quinn. That thought had barely occurred to her when Morgan stiffened, her eyes fixed on a rear door of the museum. She couldn't see clearly because of the wispy fog, but it looked like at least three men coming out—and they were carrying a fourth between them.

There was no logical reason for Morgan to assume the man being carried was Quinn. All the men were wearing dark clothing, and she was too far away to be able to spot any identifying feature. But she knew it was him, just as she knew he had been in her museum more than once watching her. *She knew.*

Frozen, she watched a dark van pull up near the men. They tossed the apparently unconscious one into the back of the van, making Morgan wince because of the rough way they treated that limp body.

God, he couldn't be dead?

She pushed that thought away instantly, refusing to consider the possibility. What she should do, she thought as she watched the three other men get into the van, was to call somebody. That was what she should do.

"911," she muttered to herself. "That's who I ought to call. Or Max. I could call Max, and tell him to get his Interpol agent out here and rescue—I mean *catch*—Quinn." She automatically started her car's engine as the van pulled away from the museum, and murmured somewhat helplessly, "Why am I not doing that?"

• • •

An hour later Morgan felt the question more intensely. What on earth was she doing? Her knowledge purely a matter of cops-and-robbers on television, she was cautiously following a van containing three probable bad guys and an internationally famous cat burglar who was either unconscious or dead. She didn't know where they were going except for the vague notion that it was south, and she was swearing at herself for a host of sins beginning with stupidity.

Tailing the van was relatively easy at first; the streets were busy, Morgan had no trouble keeping a car or two between her and the van, and she wasn't stopped once by an inconvenient traffic light. But then traffic thinned, the fog thickened, and she had to get closer than she liked to the van or risk losing it.

It was only minutes later that it pulled over to the curb, and Morgan barely had the presence of mind to continue on past the van for a full block before turning into a side street. Until then she'd paid very little attention to her surroundings, and when she did look, she couldn't help but wish she had listened to her rational side and called 911.

It hadn't been what anyone would have called a good neighborhood to begin with, and the last earthquake had made a shambles of most of the buildings Morgan could see. Obviously rebuilding wasn't high on any landlord's priority list. A dog barked somewhere off in the distance, but other than that there seemed to be no signs of life.

Swallowing, Morgan found her can of Mace in her purse, left the bag on the floorboard of the car, and got out. She locked up the car and kept her key ring in one hand with the police whistle ready—for all the good it was likely to do around here.

A few scattered streetlights cast a weird glow down through the fog, but they provided enough light for Morgan to find her way back to the van. It loomed up suddenly before her, freezing her in her tracks for a long moment until she realized there was no one in it. She checked just to make sure, but it was empty.

It was parked before a building that looked to be ten or twelve stories high, maybe an old office building, she thought. Most of the doors and windows were boarded up, and though she couldn't see it clearly, Morgan had the feeling this building had been condemned for a long time, even before the earthquake had rattled it. There was almost a smell about it, musty and disused.

Inwardly still cussing herself, she nonetheless made her way around the building with the utmost caution, looking for a way in. She found it in the rear, a warped door pulled half off its hinges, and about seven or eight stories up she saw a dim light coming from a boarded-up window. She paused for several minutes, her ears straining for any sound. She thought she heard a couple of dull thuds from up there, and once a ghostly laugh, but mostly what she heard was the frightened thudding of her heart.

She had to take several deep breaths before she could gather the courage to enter the building. It was awfully dark, even after her eyes adjusted a bit, and she had to shove her key ring and police whistle into the pocket of her jeans so she could use that hand to feel gingerly along the wall.

The floor seemed fairly solid under her feet and there didn't seem to be any obstructions of old furniture and the like to hinder her, but there were squeaks and rustles in the darkness that made Morgan grit her teeth and move a bit faster. She located a stairwell almost totally by touch, and her relief turned to wariness when she realized that there was dim light spilling down from somewhere above.

She moved with even more caution, her can of Mace held ready. Although she couldn't help but wonder how the small can would fare against three large and probably armed ruffians. Telling herself fiercely not to borrow trouble, she continued moving, always up. By the time she reached the fourth floor, she could see fairly well, and by the sixth she knew the light was only a couple of floors above her.

On the eighth floor landing she found a rusted old fire door hanging open, and just inside the hallway a battery lantern sat innocently on the floor. Morgan was tempted, but didn't pick it up. Instead she peered carefully through the doorway. She could see more light coming from a half-closed door at the end of the hallway and, when she strained, hear the indistinguishable sounds of voices.

Now what? she mouthed to herself. After a slight hesitation, she slipped through the door and into the hall. Pressing herself tightly to the wall, she made her way slowly, her eyes fixed on that partially opened door. She was more than halfway there when one voice rose harshly above the others and froze her—because it was so vicious and because she recognized it.

"It won't take us long to find out who you are. I'd kill you now, but you might come in handy for something later on. There might even be a price on your head."

And then, almost inaudible but reaching Morgan's straining ears like the sound of sweet, insouciant music, came Quinn's dry reply.

"No honor among thieves? I'm saddened, gentlemen, deeply saddened. To say nothing of being disillusioned."

"Shut up," the harsh voice ordered. "There's no way you're going to get loose, so don't bother trying. You can yell all you want; there's nobody to hear you. I'll be back in the morning when I decide what to do with you."

Morgan remained frozen for an instant longer, and then gasped and slid along the wall to the nearest door. Not only was it not locked, it didn't even have a doorknob. She pushed it open and slipped into the room, then pushed it back and pressed herself against the wall, trying to control her breathing. Within minutes she heard footsteps passing the room where she was hiding, the heavy steps of large men.

She counted to ten slowly, then very cautiously opened her door and peered down the hall toward the stairwell. They had left the lantern, which rather surprised her, but she supposed they had flashlights. She debated for a moment, but decided she could go back and get the lantern once she found out what Quinn's situation was. She was too impatient to wait any longer, hurrying down the hall toward the now closed door.

When she neared it, she noticed a large, shiny metal hasp instead of a knob on the door; it was open since there was no padlock or pin with which to lock the hasp in place over the staple. And the door itself was a metal one, set with what looked to be very solid hinges. Morgan wondered briefly what these very new bits of hardware were doing in this decrepit building—and a few possibilities garnered from thrillers on the late show made her shudder.

She was just reaching for the hasp when she heard the distant thuds of returning footsteps. Morgan looked toward the other end of the hallway, saw the flickering light of someone climbing up the stairs holding a flashlight, and felt a rush of panic. If she tried to move away from this door, she knew she would be seen; he'd be in this hallway within seconds, and the next nearest door was too far away for her to reach it in time. There was nothing else to do. Swiftly she opened the door to Quinn's prison and nipped inside, closing it gently behind her.

It was pitch-dark and utterly silent in there. Morgan, pressed against the wall by the door, held her can of Mace ready as the heavy footsteps neared the door. Then, while she waited tensely, she heard several metallic noises, the faint squeak of a hinge, and then a solid click.

The footsteps went away, leaving Morgan sagged against the wall and filled with a horrible realization. Somebody had come back with a padlock, dammit.

Wonderful. She and Quinn were on the eighth floor of a condemned building, in a room with a very businesslike locked door barring their way, and even if they could pry the boards off the windows, it was doubtful there was a fire escape.

While Morgan leaned there, silently cussing herself and Quinn, she heard a faint rustle and then a conversational voice.

"I only caught a glimpse when the door opened, but there can't be two women in this city with such a . . . distinct profile. Morgana, what are you doing here?"

She took a deep breath, relaxed her death grip on the can of Mace, and shoved it in her jeans pocket. "I happened to be in the neighborhood," she said, proud of her careless tone. It almost matched his.

"I see. Well, leaving the absurdity of that aside for the moment, do you happen to have a trusty penknife or pair of sewing scissors?"

"Not on me. From what I heard, you're tied up?"

"Afraid so. And they took all my tools." He sighed, then spoke briskly. "This room is about twenty feet square and my wretched cot is located about eight feet away from the door. If you could make your way over here and try your hand at untying these ropes, I would greatly appreciate it."

Morgan was surprised at her own calm. The only thing she could figure out was that she was in shock. So she was able to cross the room slowly, estimating the distance, until she felt the cot against her legs, and then kneel down on the hard floor beside it. Now, in which direction lay his head?

Querulously, he said, "What on earth is taking so long? All you have to do is—" He broke off with a peculiar sound.

Morgan hastily withdrew her hands, which had landed rather off target, so to speak. "Um—sorry," she murmured.

Quinn cleared his throat. "Not at all," he disclaimed politely with only a trace of hoarseness in his voice. "I've always wondered what the attraction was in being held immobile by various bindings and— uh—caressed. There is a certain appeal, I must admit. Though I would, I believe, prefer to have my own hands free should you choose to—"

"Shut up," she ordered fiercely. "It's dark in here, that's why. I can't see what I'm doing."

He sighed. "Yes, of course. Foolish of me to think otherwise."

Morgan reached out again, this time with extreme caution, and encountered the bulky shape of his tool belt. She hoped. With more confidence she felt the hard flatness of his stomach, and inched upward warily.

In a conversational tone Quinn said, "You're repaying me for having stolen your necklace, aren't you, Morgana?"

Startled, she allowed her hands to lie flat over the steady rise and fall of his chest. "What?" She'd forgotten the necklace until he mentioned it.

"This torture. Here I lie, helpless and at your mercy, while you amuse yourself with me. If it's ravishment you have in mind, I shall bear it like a man, but please take care how you fondle my poor abused body. Those cretins were not kind."

Morgan grasped the salient fact among absurdities and leaned closer as she demanded, "What did they do to you?"

"I would rather not discuss it," Quinn replied affably. "I would suggest, however, that you refrain from . . . Is that . . . ? Yes, I believe so. Even in the dark, quite obvious. Rather prominent, aren't they?"

She straightened hastily. "Quinn, do you want to get out of here alive?" she asked irately.

"I—"

"Yes or no, dammit."

"Yes."

"Then stop making crude remarks."

He cleared his throat. "Admiring remarks, Morgana. Always admiring."

The wistfulness in his too expressive voice made her want to giggle, but she overcame the ridiculous impulse. "Just shut up about my anatomy, or I'll leave you here to rot. Which is just what you deserve."

"Yes, ma'am," he murmured, not bothering to point out that both of them could rot here in the locked room, tied or not.

Morgan let her fingers resume their progress, but stopped when they encountered the warmth of his throat. She swallowed as she realized he wasn't masked, but managed to say lightly, "My kingdom for a match."

He sighed. "Sorry I can't oblige. The ropes, Morgana, please. My fingers are going numb."

She couldn't resist the temptation to glide her fingertips over his face first, feeling smooth skin over his stubborn jaw and high cheekbones, an aristocratic nose, unbelievably long lashes, a high forehead, and thick, soft hair. She tried to be quick, hoping he'd think she was merely feeling her way in sheer indifference, but then he cleared his throat again and spoke in a slightly husky but wry tone.

"If I solemnly promise never to steal anything from you again, will you stop doing that, Morgana? At least while I'm bound and helpless?"

She bit her lip to hold back a sudden giggle. "As if I'd believe your promise. Ah—here we are."

His wrists were tied to the very sturdy posts of the cot, and Morgan's amusement faded when she felt how the ropes were digging into his wrists. It was difficult to untie ropes she couldn't see, but she worked at the knots fiercely, sacrificing her fingernails and even a bit of skin from her knuckles.

"What *are* you doing here?" he asked finally while she struggled with the ropes. "I didn't see much of it, but I believe this neighborhood is a long way from yours."

Morgan didn't want to tell him the truth, but she couldn't think of a convincing lie. All she could do was make it sound more casual than it had been. "I was driving by that museum—the fine-arts one—and saw three men throw you into a van."

He didn't ask how she had known it was he. Instead he said, "So you followed them here?"

"It seemed like a good idea at the time," she answered, then made a little sound of triumph when the rope around his right wrist finally gave way.

In a judicious tone Quinn said, "Morgana, that has to be the most reckless thing I have ever heard of in my life."

"Coming from you, that is praise of a high order. Can you move your—there, like that. Just another second now, and I think— got it!"

Quinn sat up on the cot, and though she couldn't see him, she knew he was rubbing his wrists. "Thank you, Morgana."

"Are your ankles . . . ?"

"I'll get those," he said.

She sat back on her heels, wishing there was just a bit more light so she could see his face. It would be too bad, she thought, if she went through all this and was denied a glimpse of his naked face. She felt she'd earned that much.

"Quinn . . . the man who threatened to kill you, the one with the vicious voice—that was Ed, wasn't it? One of that gang of thieves who were robbing the museum the night we met?"

Untying his ankles, Quinn said, "You have a good ear."

"Then you ran into them again? Don't tell me you wound up burgling the same place?"

"Ridiculous, isn't it? And unfortunate—this time they caught me."

A bit dryly Morgan said, "If you guys keep bumping into each other like this, people will begin to talk."

He chuckled softly. "Morgana, I've missed you."

With an effort she ignored that. "You stole my one good piece of jewelry, you lousy thief. You and I have a score to settle. That is, if we ever get out of here."

The cot creaked as he moved, and she felt the brush of his legs as he swung them to the floor. "I have no intention of waiting here for the charming Ed to return. If I did, I've a feeling my next bit of publicity would be an obituary."

Morgan winced. "You could have gone all night without saying that. What's the plan?"

"To get out," Quinn replied succinctly.

"There's a padlock on the door—and it's the one door in this whole miserable building built to do its job. We're on the eighth floor. How do you propose to get out?"

"There are windows, aren't there?" He got to his feet a bit gingerly and caught his breath, muttering, "Dammit."

Morgan heard the note of pain in his voice and quickly got up herself. She reached out carefully, relieved when she touched his arm. "Are you all right?"

He let out a low laugh. "That, *chérie*, is a loaded question. Let's just say I'm functional, and leave it at that."

She let go of his arm, sensing it when he moved past her toward the faint chinks of light representing the windows. "The windows must be barred," she offered.

Quinn didn't answer for a moment, but then she heard a low, groaning creak and a satisfied sound from him. "Ah—just as I hoped. This room is designed more to keep things out than in. The metal grating over the windows swings in."

Morgan tried to remember what she'd seen of the building. Precious little, because of the fog. "But most of the windows are boarded up on the outside."

"Yeah." There was a loud thud, then another, and Quinn's powerful kick sent one of the boards flying.

The amount of light that came streaming into the room would have been pitiful under other circumstances, but to Morgan it was a veritable ray of sunshine. She blinked, moving toward it, and didn't realize until he kicked another board loose that she could see him now.

He was fair, which surprised her a bit, his hair thick and a pale color that was either gold or silver. And his face, his naked face, was visible to her for the first time. Even in the pallid, wispy light it was a good face. A strong face. It was the face she had touched. Lean and unusually handsome, with high cheekbones, a patrician nose, and those beautiful green eyes set under flying brows. It was a face Morgan knew she would never forget, no matter what happened.

It was also somewhat the worse for wear, boasting what was going to be a beautiful shiner around his right eye and another bruise high on his left cheekbone. Since she knew he'd been unconscious during part of tonight, she thought he probably had quite a headache from having been knocked out. It said something about his nature, she thought, that he could maintain his sense of humor under such conditions.

Unconscious of her scrutiny, Quinn leaned through the opening he'd made and said, "We're in luck. There's a kind of catwalk out here. If it wraps the building, we should find a fire escape or at least an open window to get us into an unlocked room."

The description filled Morgan with foreboding. When he drew back enough for her to see past him, her fears were realized. A "kind of catwalk" indeed; it looked more like one of those rickety things window washers used, except that it was affixed to the side of the building as if meant to be permanent.

"I think not," she said politely. "If you want to try it, go ahead. And if you make it, call the police and ask them to come get me, would you?"

Quinn shook his head slightly and looked at her with a serious expression. "Morgana, we have no way of knowing how much time we have here. Despite what he said Ed could have tossed a lighted match downstairs, or left one of his bullies to do it later. The place could be wired for the sole purpose of getting rid of some nasty little problem—like a witness. We can't waste any time. We have to go. Now."

She wasn't happy, but her common sense told her Quinn was right. The sooner they got out of here the better off they were bound to be. Squashing her fears and keeping her eyes fixed on his face, she said, "All right, but if you get me killed, I'll haunt you forever."

He smiled, and if his voice held charm, it was nothing compared with that crooked, beguiling smile. "Good girl. Just follow behind me—not too close, we need to distribute the weight as much as possible—and stay very close to the building."

Morgan waited while he climbed through the window and eased his weight onto the catwalk. Then, looking at him and not at anything else, she followed.

For about twenty feet all went well. Morgan was never afterward able to decide if what happened was due to the age of the building, earthquake damage, or some sick joke perpetrated by Ed or someone like him. All she knew was that their catwalk just sort of disintegrated in midair with an unthreatening little *whoosh* sound.

If she hadn't been obeying Quinn's instructions to walk close to the building, Morgan never would have been able to catch herself. As it was, she was barely able to balance herself well enough to keep from toppling off the treacherously narrow ledge that was all that was left of their catwalk.

As for Quinn, he'd been moving a little farther out, and the sudden drop of the catwalk almost got him. If he hadn't had exceptionally powerful hands with which to grip the ledge, he never would have been able to save himself.

He caught his balance with the agility of a cat and used the muscles of his arms and shoulders to pull himself up. He felt his way by touch alone, his gaze fixed unwaveringly on Morgan. She was pressed back against the wall, her slender body rigid and her head tilted slightly so that she was looking up rather than down.

"All right?" he called softly.

"Oh, I'm fine." Her voice was unnaturally calm.

Quinn frowned slightly but, satisfied that she was in no immediate danger—the section of ledge on which she was standing looked fairly solid, at least for the moment—turned his attention to their predicament. The catwalk had taken bits of the building with it when it had collapsed, depriving them of most of the pitiful ledge on which they were standing.

The ledge had given way cleanly on the other side of Morgan, which made it impossible for them to retreat to their prison even if they wanted to; on this side of her, and between their positions, at least two gaping cracks were mute evidence of instability. Climbing up to the roof would be useless; he knew from the style of what he had seen of the building that the roof would be steeply pitched and covered with fog-wet tiles that would be slippery. And though he possessed the skill and ability to rappel down, there was nothing to which a rope could be securely fastened—even if he had one.

"Don't move," he told her.

"Don't worry."

He had to smile a little at her tart response, but his sense of danger urged him to move swiftly. Testing each foothold cautiously, he eased ahead toward the corner of the building. At least twice the ledge beneath him crumbled, and he knew even before he reached it that the corner was badly cracked and unlikely to be able to hold his weight. He paused still some feet from the corner and considered rapidly.

"I'm going to climb up to the next ledge," he said finally. "All the windows on this floor are boarded up, but there may be one uncovered above us."

"Great," she said faintly.

Despite his assured statement Quinn wasn't looking forward to what he had to do. There was no way to anchor himself, and precious little to hold on to since there was no catwalk, crumbling or otherwise, for the floor above. Aside from which the building was cursed with jutting bits of stonework guaranteed to do nothing except get in his way. By reaching up, he could grasp the ledge above them, but it was smooth and slippery, offering no purchase for his grip.

It was a long way to the ground.

Quinn closed his mind to that and concentrated on necessity. He managed to turn his body, balancing sideways on the narrow ledge with his feet wide apart to distribute his weight more evenly. He reached up with both hands and carefully explored the ledge, hoping for a tiny projection that would give him a better grip. He had to take a step back toward Morgan before he found what he sought, and the ledge crumbled beneath his foot just as his fingers closed over the sharp projection.

It held. Hardly breathing, Quinn boosted himself up by using the strength of one arm, his boots scrabbling for a foothold against the side of the building, until he could get the other arm over the ledge. Moments later he was lying full-length against the building on a ledge less than a foot wide.

"Quinn?"

"Hmmm?" Still holding to his tiny projection, he rested his forehead on his arm and wondered idly how he got into situations like this one. His head was throbbing from the earlier blow, several parts of his face hurt, his wrists were raw, and he had the suspicion that at least two ribs were cracked.

Not one of his better days.

"Are you all right?" Morgan's voice was beginning to show signs of strain.

"Peachy." He lifted his head and then sat up carefully, looking around. Ah. Just as he'd hoped—an uncovered window. And it was directly above Morgan's position. "Let me get set," he said, "and I'll pull you up."

"I don't think so. I don't want to be a bother," she said conversationally, "but I feel I should mention I have this thing about heights."

Feeling relatively secure on his perch, Quinn leaned out a bit so that he could look down at her. "Now's a fine time to tell me."

"I was hoping it wouldn't come up," she murmured.

"Lousy pun."

She made an odd sound that might have been a laugh on the edge of breaking. "Unintentional, I promise you. Look—why don't you get yourself down and then send for the fire department. They have nice ladders."

Quinn didn't bother to remind her that they couldn't afford the time. Instead he slid along the ledge until he was directly above her. He had the window open in seconds, though it took considerable muscle to force the ancient sash upward. He moved as quickly as he could, virtually certain that Morgan's calm was tenuous; she had a great deal of courage, he thought, but phobias could turn even the stoutest hearts to jelly.

The room he found himself in was empty of anything he might have used to help her. He braced himself as well as he was able, then leaned out the window and across the ledge, stretching one hand down to her.

"Give me your hand, Morgana."

"Sorry. I can't move."

"You won't lose your balance. Just reach directly above your head with one hand."

"No. I'll fall."

Quinn's voice remained calm and certain. "Sweetheart, I won't let you fall. I promise. You know I keep my promises."

She was still for a moment, then slowly reached upward with her right hand until her fingers closed convulsively around his wrist. He locked his fingers around her delicate wrist, making sure he had a good grip.

"All right. I've got you. Now I want you to turn around until you're facing the wall."

"I can't do that."

"Yes, you can. Just—"

"What am I doing here?" she said in a voice of total bewilderment. "I'm on the side of a building. This is absurd. I don't do things like this."

"Of course not. Turn around and face the building, like a good girl."

Irritably she said, "I'm not a child."

"Then stop acting like one," he told her sharply. He could feel her stiffen, and a jolt of relief went through him when she began to turn around. He had infinite patience as well as genuine sympathy for her feelings, and would have hung out the window for hours if necessary—but from this position he could see a crack in the ledge between her feet, and it was widening.

She began to unbalance as she turned, but he was ready for that. It wasn't the first time he'd lifted her weight, and since she was a small woman, he had no trouble supporting her, even though his ribs gave him merry hell. And, unfortunately, Morgan's anatomy made it somewhat painful for her to be dragged over the edge of the ledge and through the window.

Several breathless moments later she was standing inside the dim room with him, half-consciously rubbing the parts of her that had been abused.

"Shall I kiss it and make it better?" Quinn asked, entirely his insouciant self again.

Morgan shrugged off his supporting arm and took a pointed step away from him. "No, you shall not." Her retort was more automatic than annoyed, and she followed it by saying sincerely, "But thanks for not leaving me out there to roost."

"It was the least I could do, since you saved my hide earlier. And now I think we should vacate this firetrap before our friends come back."

"You won't get an argument. Lead on, Macduff." She followed him in silence as he moved through the dark hall of the ninth floor toward the stairwell. Her panic out on the ledge had been the frozen kind, and with relatively solid flooring underneath her now, even the ghostly echoes of fear were gone. In any case, she was wrestling with other ghosts now.

Loyalty, for one.

Quinn had, in all probability, saved her life. Perhaps, as he'd said, he had felt that he owed her that, but the fact remained that she probably would have died without him—never mind that she wouldn't have been here in the first place if she hadn't gone haring after him. The ledge beneath her had been crumbling, she knew. He had saved her from certain death; she had merely untied him—something he probably could have done himself, given time.

She owed him. But she owed Max Bannister her loyalty.

"You're very quiet," Quinn noted as he opened the door of the stairwell and began descending with the cautious speed of a man who knows the building's unsafe.

Morgan wrestled the ghosts for two more flights downward, then sighed. Holding her voice steady, she said, "Stay away from Bannister's collection, Quinn."

He was silent for another flight, then stopped on a shadowy landing and turned to look at her. "Is there any reason aside from the obvious one why I should?"

"Yes. Because it's a trap." She drew a deep breath and gazed up at him. "There's an Interpol agent working with Max. They want to catch you."

"And the collection is bait?"

She nodded. It was difficult to make out his face, still an unfamiliar one to her, but she thought his handsome features remained expressionless.

"Why warn me, Morgana?"

"I pay my debts," she answered stiffly.

"Even if the price is loyalty?"

His soft voice was like salt rubbed in a wound, and she lifted her chin higher as she stared up at him. "I'll make peace with my conscience in my own way," she said. "And peace with Max. Maybe he'll forgive me. Maybe he won't. But I owed you something. Now we're even."

"Not quite," he said, and pulled her into his arms.

In the back of Morgan's mind was the realization that this was no sneaky distraction from a thief who wanted to steal some bauble she wore; this was something else. His powerful arms held her tightly against him so that she could feel the hardness of his body, and when his mouth covered hers, it was with the hot, sure touch of possession.

This was insane, and she knew it. She knew it when a strange, feverish tremor rippled through her body, when her arms went around his waist, when her lips parted eagerly beneath his. She knew it when she realized he had stolen more from her than a simple ruby necklace.

It was insane, and reckless, and hopelessly irrational—and Morgan didn't fight it because she couldn't.

He lifted his head at last, and his voice was a bit husky when he said, "We have to get out of here."

She nodded silently and didn't protest when he stepped back, but she felt grateful when he reached for her hand and held it the rest of the way down the stairwell. She didn't want to think at all, because she was coping with the shock of realizing that she was falling for a thief.

Quinn didn't waste any time getting them out of the building, moving swiftly but cautiously. As soon as they were outside, he said, "Where's your car?"

Morgan gestured silently and walked beside him down the block to the side street where she'd parked. He released her hand and waited while she unlocked and opened the driver's-side door. Then, softly, he said, "Get out of here, Morgana."

She blinked up at him. "You . . . ?"

"I'll be fine. You go home. And—thank you for charging to my rescue. It almost gives me hope. . . ."

She thought for a minute that he was slipping into his teasing, Don Juan persona, and she thought she would never forgive him if he did.

But then he stepped closer and bent his head to kiss her with a gentleness that made her throat ache. "I think you're going to break my heart," he murmured. Before she could respond, he had faded back into the fog and darkness of the night.

After a long moment Morgan got into her car and drove away from the shattered buildings.

Eight

By Monday morning Wolfe's fascination—or obsession—with Storm had only grown more powerful. He had spent the entire weekend with her, even keeping her with him when he needed to return to his apartment for fresh clothing. They had ended up spending several hours of Saturday afternoon in his bed and then had returned there that night simply because his apartment was closer to Candlestick Park than her hotel.

"Bear's going to feel neglected," Storm had said a bit guiltily, but since she had left plenty of food and water for her pet in the hotel—he disliked crowds, which was why he hadn't accompanied them to the baseball game—she was able to assure herself that he'd be fine alone for the night.

"I don't think he likes me," Wolfe confessed.

"He just doesn't know you, is all." Lightly Storm had added, "He's not used to having a man around."

Wolfe made an effort to charm the enigmatic cat, scratching him under the chin and feeding him bits of meat from their Sunday-night dinner in the suite, but he didn't think he'd made much of an impression. Until Monday morning. That was when he woke up in Storm's bed, with her cuddled up to his side as usual, and found the little blond cat curled up in the crook of her arm—which was flung across his chest. Wolfe had felt the most absurd sense of triumph as he'd lain there with Storm in his arms and her cat sleeping on his chest.

He hadn't wanted to disturb either of them, but since neither he nor Storm could afford to spend a weekday away from the museum with the scheduled opening of the *Mysteries Past* exhibit so near, he didn't have much choice. He'd discovered that Storm was not a morning person, resisting any attempt to wake her up for as long as possible, and he enjoyed his attempts. She was never grumpy, just sleepy and utterly limp—and he was amused to find that her cat was just the same. When he lifted Bear from his chest, the small golden cat hung from his hand as though he were boneless, enigmatic green eyes closed.

"Wake up, you ridiculous cat," Wolfe said, gently shaking the dangling handful of fur.

Sleepily Storm murmured, "He's not a morning person either."

"Well, he has to wake up. You too; I want to take you out for breakfast on the way to the museum."

She levered herself up on an elbow and peered at him, her green eyes drowsy. "Oh, God, it's Monday, isn't it?"

"Afraid so." He thought about spending eight or nine hours with her at the museum, frustrated by people coming and going all around them, and wondered if he could talk her into returning to his apartment or coming back here at lunchtime.

Storm sighed gustily. "It's going to be a long day."

Wolfe wondered if she meant it the same way he thought, but didn't ask. He slid a hand into her wild, tumbled hair and raised his head to kiss her, absently returning Bear to his chest. She was instantly, sweetly responsive, as always, and he nearly groaned when he thought of the long day ahead of them.

She smiled at him when the kiss ended, her soft lips pouty from the hungry pressure of his, and murmured, "Let's come back here for lunch."

"You're on." He hoped she'd think the raspy sound of his voice was simply due to the morning, and not to her shattering effect on him.

She pushed herself up until she was half sitting, her long hair veiling her nakedness, and Wolfe tried to distract himself before the urge to haul her back down beside him became too strong to fight. The distraction he found was Bear, who was still on his chest, sprawled out now with boneless legs and one ear folded under, snoring softly.

"He's still asleep?"

"I told you, he's not a morning person." Storm reached over and found the tip of the cat's tail, then pinched it gently.

Bear's head jerked up, his eyes blinking sleepily, and his vivid little face was such a feline replica of Storm's that Wolfe burst out laughing. Jostled a bit by the chest moving under him, Bear sort of moaned, "Yahhh," and tumbled off Wolfe to the bed beside him.

Still chuckling, Wolfe said, "I'm glad at least one of us is easy to wake up."

"All he needs is food," Storm said. "And all I need is a shower and coffee."

They shared the shower, and despite Wolfe's good intentions the steam in the stall had less to do with hot water than with their response to each other. It was the second time he had wanted her so badly that he hadn't been able to wait long enough to get them out of the shower, and since Storm was every bit as urgent, their joining was so explosive it left them drained and clinging to each other.

"Or maybe I don't need coffee," she murmured, rubbing her wet, rosy cheek against his chest.

"If we keep doing this," he told her ruefully, "what I'm going to need is a chiropractor."

"Are you complaining?"

"Hell, no."

He didn't feel like complaining about anything—except the fact that both of them had to go to work. They stopped at a small restaurant for breakfast, and Wolfe amused Storm by saving a piece of his bacon to take to the little cat waiting patiently for them in the car.

"I fed him at the hotel," she reminded.

"I know. He just looked so . . . woeful when we left him out there."

Storm chuckled. "If you let him brainwash you with those pathetic looks, he'll have you right where he wants you. Cats are the world's worst opportunists."

Wolfe didn't argue with her; he had the sheepish idea that she was right. But he took the bacon out to Bear anyway.

It was after nine when they got to the museum, and Wolfe found himself unusually conscious of the guards' impassive observation as he carried most of Storm's homework in for her. It bothered him only because those same guards had watched him, during the course of the past months, being dropped off or picked up by a succession of blondes, and he wanted to tell them this was something entirely different. Except that it wasn't any of their business anyway.

When she unlocked the door of the computer room, he carried her stuff in and piled it on the desk. "Are you going to be stuck in here all day?" he asked her.

"Pretty much," she said, smiling up at him. "I have to load all the floor plans and security hardware diagrams into the computer to form the basis of the security program, so that means I have to stay close."

He sighed. "I'll be on the phone all morning with Lloyd's. And this afternoon I need to go and talk to the police about that robbery Saturday night." The morning paper delivered to Storm's hotel suite had told them the bare facts of the robbery, but Wolfe believed he could get more information from his police contacts.

Storm had brought the paper with her since she wanted to study it more carefully, and glanced at it where it lay on her desk. "Did that museum have a modern security system?" she asked, thinking he'd know.

"Yeah, very modern. And I want to find out how they got past it."

"They?" Storm looked up at him curiously. "The article said only a few pieces of jade and ivory were stolen, and that there was no way to know who the thief was. Do you have some idea?"

Wolfe shrugged. "The way things have been vanishing in this city, you'd think we had a wandering black hole. Do I have an idea? Sure, plenty of them. But all I know for certain is that we have at least one gang of thieves operating in San Francisco and God knows how many independent contractors or collectors."

"And Quinn," Storm said.

Wolfe frowned slightly. "How did you know about him? There hasn't been any publicity about him, and I sure as hell didn't tell Ace."

Silently swearing at herself for that blunder, Storm smiled and said dryly, "Morgan told me. Correct me if I'm wrong, but since he's been in the city for weeks, apparently, and all we can be sure he's stolen is a single jeweled dagger, shouldn't he be pretty high up on our list of concerns? I mean, he must be waiting for something, and if it's *Mysteries Past* . . ."

Wolfe looked a bit grim. "Yeah, I know. That's one reason I want to talk to the cops, to find out if they have any suspicions it might have been him Saturday night. Since only a few choice pieces were taken, it sounds more like him or one of the other collectors than that gang. I need to know."

She nodded. "Makes sense. Let me know what you find out?"

"Of course." He leaned down to kiss her, ending up with both arms wrapped around her when he lifted her completely off her feet, a position Storm clearly enjoyed as much as he did. She melted against him bonelessly, and when he finally lifted his head, she gave him a smile so sensual it stopped his breathing.

Only Wolfe's awareness of likely interruptions kept him from closing and locking the door and making love to Storm right on top of her cluttered desk. Sinking fast? He was sunk.

Reluctantly he leaned back down to set her on her feet, and when he released her and straightened, he found he'd acquired a passenger.

Obviously surprised that her cat had transferred to Wolfe's shoulder from her own, Storm said, "If it bothers you, just set him on the desk."

Wolfe hesitated, but he liked the slight, warm weight of the little cat and he was still feeling a bit proud in having won over Storm's familiar. "No, it's okay. At least—he won't dig his claws in every time I move, will he?"

"Only if you startle him by moving suddenly. Actually his balance is pretty good, so he hardly needs to hold on. If he wants down, he'll tell you, and that's when you should bring him back here. I've got his litter box in here, remember."

He knew that; it was over in a corner of the room, and matched the one she kept in her hotel suite.

"I'll remember." Still he hesitated, finally bending to kiss her again, this time briefly. Dammit, he didn't want to leave her even to go to his office fifteen feet down the hall!

When he left, with a look of reluctance Storm had no trouble reading and which made her heart beat faster, she went slowly around the desk and got settled, turning on the computer and trying to arrange the clutter into some kind of order. When the computer was ready for input, she set it up to begin receiving all the data concerning specific details of the museum and the various security hardware. All that was ready to be transferred from floppy disks, which the previous computer programmer had prepared and which Storm had found to be perfectly acceptable.

While the computer began digesting data Storm eyed her telephone, mentally decided to postpone the necessary call, and drew the newspaper toward her. She was very curious about the Saturday-night robbery.

She had just read the short article through for the second time when a light voice said, "Buy you a cup of coffee?"

Her first thought was that Morgan was upset about something, though it was more a perception than a certainty. The brunette seemed both keyed up and curiously calm, as if she had dragged on a surface tranquillity to mask a deep turmoil. And it was that more than anything else which caused Storm to agree affably and accept the cup Morgan had brought with her.

"Thanks. Have a seat," she invited.

The computer room's one visitor's chair was shoved over into a corner to be out of the way, so Morgan casually sat on the edge of the big desk. "Where's your cat?" she asked.

"With Wolfe."

"Oh-ho. Is that as promising as I think it is?"

Storm widened her eyes innocently.

Smiling slightly, Morgan said, "Listen, I know it's none of my business, but I've got to know. When he went tearing out of here Friday after I delivered your message, Wolfe was madder than I've ever seen him. He looked like he wanted to strangle you. Or something."

Clearing her throat, Storm murmured, "He didn't strangle me."

"So I see. Would I be far off in assuming that you two spent the weekend together?"

"Let's put it this way," Storm said. "When Wolfe woke up this morning—Bear was on his chest."

"Do I offer congratulations?" Morgan asked solemnly.

"Not just yet. We have a few hurdles to get over before anything's settled."

A bit dryly Morgan said, "Some of his past ladies had pets, and believe me, Wolfe kept his distance. He didn't want to get involved, and it showed. If he's wearing your cat on his shoulder, it's just a matter of time."

Storm had felt hopeful about that herself, but since the hurdles looming ahead were bad ones, she didn't let herself hope too much. With a slight shrug she said, "Maybe. But speaking of his past ladies, did you see Nyssa Armstrong leave here on Friday?"

"No, why?"

"It's kind of a funny thing." Storm hesitated, but she didn't see any reason not to tell Morgan about it. "Wolfe and I went to Candlestick Park Saturday night, and I could have sworn I saw her in the crowd."

"Nyssa? At a *baseball* game?"

"Like I said—kind of funny, huh? There was a home run hit just then that distracted me, and when I looked again, I couldn't see her. But I'm pretty sure it was her. I didn't tell Wolfe, but I wondered about it."

In a theatrical tone that would have shamed one of those old radio thrillers, Morgan said, "She's obviously following you. Slinking along on your trail, bitter and heartbroken because you lured Wolfe from her bed. She's probably sharpening her knife even as we speak, her serial-killer eyes glittering with insane rage and jealousy while she plots how best to slay you and get away with it."

Storm blinked and then giggled. "Yeah, right."

Morgan grinned at her. "Hey, don't scoff. I read a book just last week where that was the killer's motive. She got away with it too. Better watch your back."

Storm shook her head and tapped the newspaper still lying open on her desk. "This is the kind of crime I'm more concerned with at the moment. Did you hear about it?"

"The robbery? Yeah, I heard about it."

"Wolfe thinks it might have been Quinn," Storm ventured, watching the other woman carefully because she sensed more than saw Morgan tense. "How about you?"

Morgan peered into her coffee cup and pursed her lips slightly, the picture of frowning concentration. "No, I don't think it was him."

"Why not?"

Amber eyes flicked toward Storm, then away again, and instead of answering, Morgan said, "I met him, you know. Quinn. A few weeks ago."

"Did you?" Storm waited a moment, then added quietly, "I'm a good listener. And I don't tell tales out of school."

"I always liked that phrase," Morgan said with a brief smile. "Telling tales out of school . . . It makes secrets sound like innocent things."

"But sometimes they aren't," Storm murmured. "Sometimes they're dangerous."

"Yeah." Morgan sighed, then set her coffee cup down on the desk. Then, quickly and somewhat tersely, she told Storm about her first late-night meeting with an infamous cat burglar named Quinn several weeks before. About him stealing her ruby necklace right off her neck—though she didn't go into detail about *that.* And, finally, about what had happened on Saturday night. Everything except for what Morgan had overheard here in the museum and those final few minutes with Quinn.

Storm drew a deep breath and murmured, "Wow. You're a braver man than I am, Gunga Din."

"Actually I was terrified. I don't know what possessed me to do such a ridiculous, dangerous thing." Morgan frowned down at her coffee cup, one hand toying with the handle. "So, anyway, I know it wasn't him that robbed the fine-arts museum Saturday night. I mean, he was obviously *going* to, but that gang got in his way . . . or whatever."

Storm leaned back in her chair and folded her hands over her stomach as she watched the other woman. "Sort of reminds me of something I once read about Byron," she said.

Her lazy drawl made the name sound curiously exotic, and it took a moment for Morgan to realize her friend meant the English poet. "Byron? You're comparing Quinn to Lord Byron?"

Storm smiled. "It's something somebody once said about Byron. Don't remember who, but it must've been a woman. She said Byron was 'mad, bad, and dangerous to know.' That sounds a lot like your Quinn."

"He isn't mine," Morgan denied automatically. But then she remembered his last words, and a little shiver went through her. Absurd, of course. It had just been another of his Don Juan lines designed to throw her off balance. She'd need her head examined if she took anything that despicable thief said seriously.

"If you say so," Storm murmured.

Morgan eyed her, then sighed. "The point is, Quinn's definitely in San Francisco. That's really what I came in here to tell you." What she wanted to do was to ask Storm if her computer system was being geared toward capturing Quinn, but she didn't dare. Having discovered the plan by eavesdropping, Morgan was very hesitant to betray knowledge of what was going on. Besides that, she couldn't be sure who else—aside from Max and the Interpol agent—was really involved in this.

If Wolfe was involved, he must have decided to take his orders solely from Max rather than Lloyd's of London, because the insurance company would certainly be wild if they found out the priceless collection they insured was being used as bait. But that was possible because Max and Wolfe were half brothers and blood was thicker than employment. If *Storm* knew, then that must mean that Ace Security was also involved, which seemed unlikely.

The problem was, Morgan decided, she couldn't really ask anybody except Max what was going on. And that meant she'd have to confess her eavesdropping to him. It also meant that somewhere along the way she would have to confess to Max that she'd also warned Quinn about the trap. But maybe she could put that off for a while. . . .

"Since he's in town," Storm was saying calmly, "he's bound to be interested in the collection. Is that why you told me? So I'd keep it in mind while I'm writing the program?"

Morgan shrugged. "I figured it couldn't hurt." She picked up her coffee cup and sipped the cooling liquid. "By the way, Max is back in town. He stopped by here after hours on Saturday to look over the exhibit wing. I haven't talked to him."

"Then I better get busy," Storm said, "and earn my pay."

Removing herself from the desk, Morgan said, "You and me both. See you later."

"You bet." Storm sat there for a long moment after the brunette had gone, then got up and went to shut the door. When she returned to her desk, she paused only to feed another floppy disk into the computer before drawing the phone toward her and picking up the receiver.

He answered on the first ring, and his, "Yeah," was impatient.

"It's me," she said.

"We have to meet," he said. "Today."

Storm sighed. "That's not going to be easy. It'll be impossible before lunchtime, I know that."

"How about during lunch?"

She felt her face get hot as she remembered her suggestion to Wolfe that they return to her suite for lunch, and his prompt agreement. Despite the passionate shower that had followed, Storm had a strong feeling they'd still go back to her hotel for something other than lunch. Food would be an afterthought.

"Storm?"

She cleared her throat. "I don't think so. Look, Wolfe said he'd probably go talk to the police sometime after lunch about the robbery Saturday night. Maybe then. But I didn't drive my Jeep this morning, so I'd have to take a cab."

He swore softly. "I don't know how much time we've got."

Storm murmured, "I wish I had a little more."

After a moment he said, "The longer this goes on, the worse it's going to be. You know that."

She knew that. "I'll call you when Wolfe leaves the museum, and we can arrange to meet. All right?"

"Yeah, all right."

She cradled the receiver gently and sat staring across the room blindly. Hurdles—God. They were walls, giant stone walls she couldn't get over or around. She was lying to the man she loved, and she was terrified he'd never forgive her for it.

• • • •

When Wolfe finally left the museum to talk to the police, it was much later than he'd planned. Lunch with Storm had been the most incredibly tempestuous, passionate hour they had yet spent together; he had the distinct feeling that if he hadn't been before, he was now most certainly marked, branded visibly for all the world to see.

He remembered how Max had looked when he'd fallen in love with Dinah, how his feelings had shown even on a face designed by nature to hide every emotion, and Wolfe wondered how Storm could possibly not know he loved her. She didn't seem to. Or maybe, he thought, she *did* know—and chose to ignore it.

That possibility bothered him so much that he delayed leaving the museum, occupying himself with unnecessary paperwork and visiting the computer room half a dozen times. Sometimes he had the excuse of bringing Bear back to use his litter box, though the little cat's bewilderment on at least two visits made that excuse suspect.

He was afraid he was making a nuisance of himself, even though Storm always seemed happy to see him. Still, despite her obvious enjoyment, he had the unsettling feeling that she was farther away from him than she had been, a little remote despite their passionate lunch, and he was going crazy trying to figure out why. Was it because his feelings were so obvious? Was Storm easing away from him mentally or emotionally because his love was something she didn't want?

Worried but unwilling to take the chance of pushing her for an answer, he finally decided to go and talk to the police. He invited her to come along with him, but she said she had at least another hour's work ahead of her and she really wanted to get it out of the way—

why not get it done while he was busy with the police? It was nearly six by then; she said if he didn't return to the museum by the time she finished, she and Bear would take a cab back to her hotel.

Wolfe had the uneasy feeling that she wanted him to go away for a while, but chalked it up to paranoia. And he didn't leave before making definite plans with her to go out to dinner as soon as he finished with the police.

But by the time he got out to his car, he was having second thoughts. He pulled out of the side parking lot and over to the curb, gazing toward the museum, trying to gain control over his growing sense of worry. A heavy overcast and creeping fog made it darker than usual for the time of day, which meant he couldn't see a great deal clearly beyond the lighted backdrop of the lobby. Nobody was going into the museum because it was so late, but visitors were beginning to stream out as closing time neared.

When a cab pulled up to the steps, Wolfe didn't think very much about it. He watched idly, drumming his fingers against the steering wheel while he told himself repeatedly that it was probably quite normal for a man in love to be filled with the most ridiculous thoughts and worries. He'd have to ask Max one day if it had been this way with him.

When she came out of the museum and went toward the cab, Wolfe felt a moment of simple surprise. A glance at his watch told him he'd been sitting out here no more than ten minutes, which meant Storm shouldn't have been able to finish the work so quickly. He started to lean on his horn to get her attention, but something, some vague suspicion, made him change his mind.

He waited to make certain the cab was moving in the opposite direction—away from Storm's hotel—and then pulled his car away from the curb and began following at a discreet distance. It wasn't a very long trip; less than fifteen minutes later, Storm's cab stopped at a small park.

Wolfe pulled to the curb the moment the cab did, and instantly killed his lights and engine. He watched, feeling peculiarly cold, as Storm got out and began walking down a narrow sidewalk that led toward a silent carousel in the distance; Wolfe knew it was there because he knew this park, but he couldn't see it because of the growing darkness and fog. He watched the cab pull away, waited a few seconds, then got out of his car and followed the same path Storm had taken.

In nearly fifteen years in the security business, Wolfe had picked up quite a number of useful things, one of which was the ability to follow someone on foot without betraying his presence. He used that ability now. As silent as a shadow, he glided along after Storm. The building that housed the huge, silent carousel was normally locked; Wolfe was close enough to see that Storm entered through a door standing open invitingly.

He hesitated, but the dim light he could see was coming from deeper in the building, so he felt safe in slipping inside after her. He moved instantly into the shadows cast by the carousel, his gaze fixed past the colorful animals to the two people standing on the other side.

"Where is he?" Storm asked quietly after a quick look around.

"On his way. You didn't give either of us much time to get here." Jared Chavalier shrugged and dug his hands into the pockets of his dark raincoat. There was a battery lantern sitting on the carousel near him, providing decent light for that section of the building.

"I don't have much time," Storm said. "Wolfe's supposed to pick me up in another hour or two for dinner. You have to make a decision about this."

"I know, I know." Jared sighed. "He's asking questions, good ones, and I can't stall him forever."

As he walked slowly around the carousel toward them, Wolfe said coldly, "Then why not try the truth?" His gaze was fixed on Storm, and even in the low light he saw her go deathly pale at the first sound of his voice. She turned slowly toward him, and he could see that the only color in her face was in the darkened green eyes. Bear was on her shoulder, his face as still as hers, and for the first time the sight of the little blond cat riding on the shoulder of the delicate blond woman had no power to soften anything inside Wolfe.

"Take it easy—" Jared began, but Wolfe ignored him and spoke directly to Storm.

"You lied to me." His voice grated, like a steel file over stone.

She didn't flinch, but though her chin lifted a bit, it wasn't with the fearless spirit he'd come to know and appreciate. And her voice held an alien note of hopelessness. Of defeat. "Yes, I lied to you. About the job. About what I came here to do."

Wolfe waited, but she offered no reasons, no excuses. She just gazed up at him with that remote face and those blank eyes. All he could think of was how honest those eyes had seemed to him, and he thought the pain and rage would tear him apart.

"What else did you lie about?" he demanded bitterly. And when she remained silent, he jerked his head toward Jared. "Was it his idea or yours to make the ultimate sacrifice, Storm? Tell me, I'm curious. Did you at least get a bonus out of it?"

Jared's voice dropped deliberately into the awful silence, every word like a stone. "If you say one more word, I swear to God I'll deck you."

But it was Storm who ended the confrontation, walking past Wolfe silently, the remoteness of her face shattered by pain. She didn't look back.

Wolfe swung around and took a hasty step after her, but brought himself up short. His heart was thudding sickly in his chest as he watched her vanish out the door, and he couldn't seem to draw a breath without feeling a stabbing agony. The rage had gone, draining away so quickly it left him empty.

Dear God, what had he done?

The silence behind him was so thick it practically touched him. When he turned slowly, he found Jared standing with his arms crossed over his chest, the strange, pale aqua eyes glittering with anger.

"Nice going, pal," he said bleakly.

Before Wolfe could respond, Jared looked past him as a movement caught his attention, and Max walked quietly out of the shadows to join them. His hard face gave little away, but it was clear he was very disturbed.

To Wolfe he said, "If you want to hit somebody, it better be me. I'm to blame for this."

"Too late," Jared muttered. "He's already beaten up his victim."

Storm wasn't thinking at all when she walked away from the carousel. She'd known it would be bad, but she hadn't expected it to hurt this much. Dimly she wondered how it was possible to function, to walk and flag down a cab and get inside and give the address of her hotel, all the time filled with this terrible grief. It was like she'd received some mortal wound, but her body hadn't recognized it yet because it was in shock.

At her hotel she walked through the big, quiet lobby and got on the elevator, more or less blind and deaf. Bear murmured nervously in her ear, but she didn't really hear him. When she got off the elevator on her floor and walked to the door of her suite, she was vaguely aware of claws digging into her shoulder, but she still didn't heed her cat.

It wasn't until she unlocked the door and opened it that Storm was jarred from her misery. A hard shove in the middle of her back propelled her into the suite so roughly that she nearly fell. Bear jumped off her shoulder and fled underneath the couch with a hiss of fear, and Storm caught her balance just in time to keep from sprawling out on the carpet.

She turned slowly, the pain inside her pushed aside for the moment by the ancient instincts of self-preservation. Her mind was clear and cold, and the first thing she took note of was the businesslike automatic in Nyssa Armstrong's slender and beautifully manicured hand.

The second thing she noticed was the insane rage gleaming in those wide blue eyes.

Oh, Morgan, you were more prophetic than we could have imagined . . .

Since Storm was a technical specialist with Interpol rather than a field agent, training aimed at coping with a situation like this one had been rather sketchy. She could defend herself physically quite well—thanks to a father and six older brothers who'd made sure she could handle herself—but she didn't know how to disarm an enemy and she wished she'd paid more attention in her few psychology classes.

"Can we talk about this?" she asked, keeping her voice as even and casual as possible.

Nyssa had allowed the suite door to close behind her. She stood just a few feet from Storm, the gun pointed unerringly at the smaller woman's chest. She was smiling. "I don't think so," she said in a reflective tone. "You see, I really do hate to lose. And if I don't stop you, I'll lose twice. First Wolfe, and then the collection."

Storm felt a chill unlike anything she'd ever experienced before. What Nyssa said was scary enough, but the way she said it was terrifying. With absolutely no sign of mockery she was imitating

Storm's Southern accent, her head slightly tilted to one side as if to listen to her own efforts.

Storm wiped the accent from her voice. "As far as the collection goes—"

"No, don't do that." Nyssa frowned at her. "I have to get the voice right. I've seen his face when you talk to him, so I know he likes the voice." She cocked the pistol. "If you don't help me, I'll kill you here."

Anything for a little more time, Storm thought. Staying alive was the first priority. "Anything you say," she drawled. "Would you like me to talk? My pleasure. Besides, I'm curious. How could you lose the collection because of me? It doesn't belong to me or to Wolfe—it belongs to Max Bannister."

Nyssa had her head tilted again, listening, and when she answered, it was with a creditable Southern accent as well as a tone eerily like Storm's. "I could have persuaded Wolfe to let me see the collection. And after that, it would have been easy to get the security details from him. I could do that, you know. Men tell me all kinds of things in bed. He would have, too, in time."

"Then you would have tried to . . . take the collection?" Storm asked, wording the question carefully. She wanted to keep the conversation away from Wolfe, if possible, because she had the instinctive certainty he was the danger zone.

"My men would have." Proudly she said, "I taught them well. The police don't have a clue."

"You mean—that gang of thieves everybody's after is under your control?" Storm was honestly astonished. Interpol had been suspicious of Nyssa, but not for that.

She laughed softly. "It's the perfect arrangement. I find out all the security details, and then they go in. I select a few choice items for myself, and give them the rest to sell to a few other collectors on their list. Everybody's happy." She was still drawling.

"It does sound efficient," Storm agreed.

Nyssa glanced at her watch. "I think we'd better be going. He'll come back here tonight, won't he? To be with you, like he was all weekend."

Before Storm could reply one way or the other, the taller blonde was going on, her voice beginning to tighten and lose a bit of its lazy drawl.

"That's when I knew for sure that I had to get rid of you. I didn't like the way he looked at you that first night, in the restaurant—as if he couldn't take his eyes off you. But I thought he'd lose interest soon. Then, at the museum on Friday, he gave me the brush-off." Her laugh was high and brittle. "Oh, he was smooth about it, but what he meant was he just wasn't interested in me anymore. It was you. I followed him over here, so I know he spent the night with you. I know he spent the entire weekend with you."

"Nyssa—"

She sort of shook her head, visibly reaching for control, and when she spoke, she was drawling again. "He's the first one I really wanted," she murmured, as if to herself. "Don't know why, just something about him."

Desperately Storm said, "I'm curious again. Did you follow me tonight, or what?"

Nyssa frowned. "No. I had something to do, so I couldn't wait outside the museum for you. I was lucky, though, because I got here just when you did. And when I saw he wasn't with you, I knew I could do it tonight. We're leaving now."

It didn't require any training or special knowledge for Storm to recognize the implacable expression on the other woman's face, or the madness in her eyes. All Storm could think of was that she would have to make some kind of move between here and the front door of the hotel; once she was out of the lobby, her chances of getting help diminished rapidly.

She didn't attempt anything as she walked slightly ahead of Nyssa out of the suite and down the hall to the elevator. The car was deserted when it stopped for them, so Storm bided her time, silently hoping there would be people in the lobby; it was usually pretty active, and there were groupings of chairs and huge planters and other places to hide.

But what if Nyssa began shooting? Could she risk that? Storm asked herself desperately. Could she be responsible for this madwoman hurting or even killing some innocent bystander? God, she *couldn't* let that happen. . . .

Frozen inside, her instincts screaming for her to do something and her mind telling her she couldn't, Storm stepped out of the elevator. Nyssa was a half step behind, a scarf draped over her hand to hide the gun that was pressing into Storm's back. They were halfway across the fairly busy lobby when a quiet voice behind Nyssa spoke her name.

To Storm the next minute or so seemed to drag out until it lasted hours. She flinched away from the gun as Nyssa jerked it away from her back, and she had to turn around just as the other woman did because it had been Wolfe's voice.

He was there, standing very still, looking at Nyssa's face rather than at the gun now aimed at him. Storm wanted to scream out a warning, but a powerful hand was pulling her away. She knew it was Max, because she could see Jared slipping up on the other side of Nyssa, his unusual eyes coldly intent.

"It's me you really want, isn't it?" Nyssa said to Wolfe in that drawling voice uncannily like Storm's. "I'll forgive you, darling, just say you don't want her anymore."

Wolfe never had to respond to that, which was probably just as well; he looked a bit sick. Before Nyssa could take in his expression, Jared made his move. He got the gun out of her hand without a wasted second, and before Nyssa could even begin to struggle, she found herself in a hold she couldn't escape.

By the time she began screaming, the police had arrived.

Nine

Storm didn't look at any of the three tall men standing in her hotel suite. Instead she gazed at the nervous little blond cat in her lap and stroked him gently. Max had brought her back to her suite soon after the police had arrived; Wolfe and Jared had joined them up here a few minutes later. She was dimly aware that they had talked, the three of them, but she had no idea what about.

Max had apologized to her quietly and sincerely, saying it was his fault she'd been put into the position of having to lie to Wolfe. It was ironic, he'd said; if she hadn't been so honest and conscientious, she would have saved herself a lot of pain by telling Wolfe the truth when their involvement became personal. Instead, bound by her sense of responsibility to do her job and obey her superior, she had been forced to go on lying.

Storm doubted that Wolfe would see it that way.

With the threat of Nyssa gone, her rush of adrenaline had gone as well, leaving her as numbly miserable as she had been before. She wasn't even interested enough to ask someone how they had known about Nyssa. They must have known; otherwise they wouldn't have been waiting in the lobby, she thought. Not that it mattered.

After an indeterminate while her frozen senses thawed enough for her to realize that Max and

Jared were leaving. She looked up, watching them go. Wolfe shut the door behind them. He was staying, she realized. He took his jacket off and flung it toward a chair without looking to see where it landed. He came toward her with a very deliberate tread. She watched him come toward her, and some instinct rather than knowledge told her he was so tense he was on the knife edge of doing something violent.

He bent down, lifted Bear out of her lap, and set him on the couch beside her, and then he jerked her up into his arms.

For a moment, the breath knocked from her by the collision with his hard chest and the strength of his arms, and more than a little dazed by his action, Storm didn't even hear the words he muttered roughly into her hair. When she did hear them, she was afraid to believe what she heard.

"God, baby, I'm sorry! I didn't mean what I said, I swear I didn't. . . . I know you'd never give yourself to any man as part of a lie, or for any reason that wasn't right. . . ."

Her arms crept around his waist, and Storm leaned back far enough to look at him when he finally raised his head. There was something wild in his eyes, and she felt hypnotized by it. "I didn't lie about that," she whispered. "What I felt when you touched me . . . How badly I wanted you. I didn't mean for it to happen, Wolfe, but I couldn't help it. And I couldn't tell you the truth about that, about how I felt, when I was lying about why I was here. . . ."

He surrounded her face in his hands, those fierce eyes even wilder. "Tell me now," he urged in a strained, raspy voice.

Storm didn't hesitate. As long as there was a chance he could forgive her, she was willing to gamble everything she had, every shred of pride and every ounce of dignity. With simple honesty she said, "I fell in love with you that first day, when

I looked up and saw you standing there glowering in such a thunderously bad mood—"

Wolfe made a hoarse sound and kissed her, his emotions too intense to allow for gentleness. Her instant response was passionate and sweet, and it shook him the way it always did because what he felt for her was so overwhelming. "I love you," he groaned, kissing her again and again.

Storm's tension drained away, and she melted against him with a wild little sound of her own. It was so wonderful she could hardly believe it possible that he loved her, but she could feel it in him now, so unrestrained, elated, and intense that he trembled with the force of it, and all her love for him rose up in her to match that force.

She didn't know how much time passed, lost in murmured words of love and insatiable kisses, but gradually she realized that Wolfe was on the couch and she was on his lap, held tightly in his arms. The position was amazingly comfortable, and she cuddled closer with a sigh of contentment even as her mind began functioning with something approaching normality.

Quietly she said, "I never wanted to lie to you, Wolfe."

"I know." He matched her tone, his own voice still a little strained. "Even before you left the carousel, I knew. Then Max was there, and between them, he and Jared explained why they'd decided to keep their plans from me."

Storm drew back a little and gazed at him gravely. "Jared didn't tell me everything, of course. He just said Max didn't want you to feel torn between loyalty to him and your responsibilities to Lloyd's. He said your job was to protect the collection, and since that wouldn't change no matter what they planned, there was no reason for you to know."

Wolfe smiled slightly, but it was a wry smile. "Both of them knew better."

"I thought they *should* have—but it wasn't my place to say," she agreed. "It seemed to me all they really wanted was to delay you finding out long enough for them to think of a good enough reason to persuade you that using the collection to bait a trap was the right thing to do."

"I think you're right," he murmured.

"Even so, when I realized how I felt about you, it put me squarely between a rock and a hard place. Interpol recruited me in college—they needed technical specialists, and with a major in computer programming and a minor in law, I was just what they were looking for—and I'd never disobeyed orders. So there was Jared saying he didn't want you to have the chance to look over the program I was writing, and I was falling for you so hard I had all the caution and subtlety of a comet—"

Wolfe kissed her, then said, "I gather your program has one of those doors we talked about a million years ago? Big enough to admit a thief?"

"Well, *one* of my programs does. I'm writing two, exactly alike except one of them has a weak spot—or door. That one's the lure, of course, put on file at Ace."

"I wondered when we'd get around to Ace," Wolfe said with visible satisfaction. "I always knew there was something fishy about Max's faith in the place."

Storm was a bit startled. "You mean, they left me to tell you all this?"

"They're rotten to the core, both of them," Wolfe said promptly. Then he smiled faintly. "To tell the truth, I wasn't in much shape to talk about it. I know some, but not all. So tell me—what's the deal with Ace?"

She cleared her throat. "I guess you didn't know Max owned the company?"

He stared at her. "No."

Storm was glad that particular lie—by omission, at least—wasn't hers. And she wondered if this was why the other two men had left her to fill in the blank spaces. Keeping her voice casual, she said, "Yeah, he does. When they decided to use the collection as bait, Jared put a couple of people inside Ace as a kind of sting. They were supposed to be amenable to bribery, which was how my fake program was going to be available as part of the lure."

"Wait a minute," Wolfe said, frowning. "There was an employee fired for breaking into secure files—"

Storm nodded. "That was unplanned, and genuine. See, Jared was still in the process of getting his people settled into the company; nothing was supposed to be happening. Nobody counted on a thief trying to get into the museum before the exhibit was in place."

Including Wolfe. "Yeah, I remember. The main thing that did was to make me concerned about Ace."

"Which was the last thing anybody wanted," Storm said dryly.

"Was the computer foul-up deliberate?"

She chuckled. "Actually, no. What was supposed to happen was that the technician was going to get most of the basic programming in place and then admit he was in over his head. He'd leave with abject apologies, and Ace would send me in. I *was* in Paris, by the way, working on another project."

"But not for Ace," Wolfe murmured.

"No."

"So what happened?"

"That poor kid really fouled up," Storm said ruefully. "Then you hit the ceiling and started raining fire and brimstone on Ace, and everybody— I mean Jared and Max—started getting nervous that you were going to throw a spanner in the works and demand a different security company. So I was rushed in and ordered to fix up Ace's black eye in a hurry. I was supposed to convince you

I was the best *and* divert your attention away from Ace."

"So your cocky attitude that first day was for show?"

She looked a bit self-conscious. "Well, no. That was really me. When you're little, you learn to talk big—especially with six older brothers."

Wolfe grinned at her. "That's a relief. In case you didn't know, one of the reasons I fell in love with you was that confident, fearless manner."

"You were just happy to have somebody who'd fight with you," Storm said, but she was pleased nonetheless.

"That too." He concentrated on the conversation. "Let's see now. . . . Oh, yeah—the phone patch."

Obediently she said, "Was supposed to be another diversion for you, if needed. Jared thought I used it too soon, and he was horrified when I pointed you at Nyssa."

"Why?"

"About Nyssa?" Storm sighed. "It's so convoluted. See, one of the inside men at Ace *had* leaked information—to Nyssa. The trap wasn't intended for her, but she's been on Interpol's watch list for years and the agent knew it. He leaked something he didn't think was very vital, intending it to draw her back again later."

It only took Wolfe a moment. "He leaked the information about you."

"Right. So she approaches me in the ladies' room to tell me she knows I'm the new computer technician, and I find myself with a potential problem. Since she also tells me how cozy you two are, I have to assume she might well share her information with you—and at this point I don't know what else was leaked to her. No matter what she tells you, it's going to turn your angry attention right back to Ace. So I decide to—take the bull by the horns. *I* tell you she's somehow found out about me, and at the same time do my best to convince you she couldn't possibly have found that out from anybody at Ace."

"You have a devious mind," Wolfe told her.

"Thank you. But Jared was convinced if your attention was on Nyssa, you'd eventually work your way back to Ace, so he wasn't happy with me."

"He also knew she was unbalanced," Wolfe said with a touch of grimness.

"He did? How?"

"Storm, she was on the Interpol watch list because at least three couriers supposedly carrying artworks from her to buyers turned up dead—with the valuables gone. Nyssa was the only common denominator in all three cases."

She shivered. "I'm glad I didn't know that. By the way, how did you guys turn up here in the nick of time?"

"That's the only reason I'm still speaking to Jared. The man he had watching Nyssa radioed that she'd followed you into the hotel."

Storm didn't want either of them to dwell on what had happened, so she said calmly, "Well, I certainly hope all this has cured you of Barbie dolls once and for all."

"You could say that," he murmured. "In fact, I've discovered a new passion."

She eyed him. "Oh, yes?"

"Definitely. I fully expect it to occupy all my attention for the next forty or fifty years."

Storm went very still, her eyes huge and uncertain, and Wolfe pulled her a bit closer. He thought he'd never seen anything as beautiful as she was, and he loved her so much his voice shook with it when he said, "I know a lot's happened in the past week, but I've never been more sure of anything in my life. I love you, Storm, more than I'll ever be able to tell you. Please say you'll marry me."

Always unexpected, Storm let out a squeal of pure delight and more or less attacked him.

Which was, Wolfe thought a long time later when he was able to think again, the best reply to a proposal any man could ever hope to have.

On Wednesday evening of that same week Wolfe left Storm at her hotel and returned to his apartment to change because they were going to have dinner with Max and Dinah. The only reason Storm hadn't yet moved in with him was because they were looking for an apartment or house with a garden where Bear could chase bugs and sun himself; in the meantime they tended to spend the night in whichever place was closest or most convenient.

Wolfe was in a good mood when he came out of his bedroom dressed for the evening, but he tensed a bit when he saw that he had a visitor—though he might have admitted to feeling a certain amount of relief.

Standing by the open window, which was obviously how he'd entered the fourth-floor apartment, and dressed all in black but unmasked, the visitor said mildly, "Got your summons. Really, though, Wolfe—an ad in the personals column?"

"Last I heard," Wolfe answered in a voice of dangerous calm, "you didn't have a permanent address."

"True enough." Quinn's voice was still mild, but his green eyes were watchful—and the open window was close enough for a quick escape if necessary. "But—you're obviously going out. Why don't I come back another time?"

"Don't you move."

Quinn winced at the fierceness in that command. "It was just a suggestion. I wouldn't have vanished off the face of the earth, you know."

"You did in London."

"That was different. I got the distinct feeling at the time that you were about to do something we'd both have been sorry for, so I cleared out. Removed temptation, so to speak."

Waving that aside with an abrupt gesture, Wolfe studied his visitor through narrowed eyes. "You look like hell," he said, taking note of assorted bruises and a lovely shiner that marred that handsome face.

"Thank you so much."

"Well, what did you expect me to say? Welcome to the States? I don't think so. I want to know what you're doing here. And I want the truth."

After a silence, during which he seemed to be weighing Wolfe's determination, Quinn sighed. "All right, but the answer won't make your life any easier."

On Friday morning of that week Morgan came into the computer room with something of a flounce, and collapsed into the visitor's chair after dragging it out of its corner.

Storm stopped typing her new security program into the computer and rested an elbow on the desk, studying the brunette thoughtfully. "You look a bit aggrieved," she said.

Morgan drew a breath, then began speaking rapidly. "When I woke up this morning, I found a gaily wrapped little package dangling from my doorknob. The *inside* of the doorknob. The door was double-locked, mind you, with dead bolts. But did that stop him? Oh, no."

"Quinn?" Storm guessed.

Morgan produced a small, ring-sized box, which she shoved across the desk at her friend. "Look at that. A copy, of course, but a damned good one. That lousy thief has taste, I'll give him that."

Opening the box, Storm found a spectacular ring with a huge, square stone that gleamed like moonlight. "It's gorgeous," she said admiringly.

Morgan scowled. "It's a nail in his coffin."

"Why?"

"There's an entire collection of them in an Eastern museum," Morgan said, almost steaming visibly. "He knew I'd recognize it. He knew. He did it deliberately, just to taunt me. And to think, I was actually beginning to believe . . . Well, never mind about that. The point is—"

"Morgan?"

"What?"

Storm held the ring box up and tapped the stone with a questioning finger. "Tell me what this is?"

"It's a *concubine* ring!" Morgan all but wailed. "That lousy, no-good, rotten excuse for a man sent me a ring they used to pass out in harems!"

While her friend began chuckling Morgan made a fierce silent promise to herself. The next time she met up with that green-eyed devil she was going to kick him where it hurt.

Hard.

Author's Note

I hope you enjoyed *Hunting the Wolfe*, the second story in my *Men of Mysteries Past* series for Loveswept.

Next is *The Trouble with Jared*, in which the cool Interpol agent finds himself faced with a lovely and haunting lady out of his past—and a shadowy watcher with a deadly purpose.

And Quinn? Well, since he and Morgan seem fated to encounter each other, you probably won't be surprised to find him turning up yet again. But next time, you may be surprised *why*. . . .

* * *

P.S. When I wrote *Hunting the Wolfe*, the Giants were still in San Francisco; heaven knows where they are now. . . .

THE EDITOR'S CORNER

There's no better way to get into the springtime mood than to read the six fabulous LOVESWEPTs coming your way. Humorous and serious, sexy and tender, with heroes and heroines you'll long remember, these novels are guaranteed to turn May into a merry month indeed.

Leading this great lineup is Linda Jenkins with **TALL ORDER**, LOVESWEPT #612. At 6'7", Gray Kincaid is certainly one long, tall hunk, just the kind of man statuesque Garnet Brindisi has been waiting for. And with her flamboyant, feisty manner, she's just the one-woman heat wave who can finally melt the cool reserve of the ex-basketball star called the Iceman. . . . Linda's writing makes the courtship between this unlikely couple a very exciting one to follow.

Please welcome Janis Reams Hudson, bestselling and award-winning author of historical and contemporary romances, and her first LOVESWEPT, **TRUTH OR DARE**, #613. In this touching story, Rachel Fredrick dons a shapeless dress, wig, and glasses, convinced the disguise will forever hide her real identity—and notorious past. She doesn't count on her boss, Jared Morgan, discovering the truth and daring her to let him heal her pain. Enjoy one of New Faces of '93!

STROKE BY STROKE, LOVESWEPT #614 by Patt Bucheister, is how Turner Knight wants to convince Emma Valerian she's the only woman for him. For two years she's been the best paralegal Turner has ever worked with—but the way his body heats up whenever she walks into his office has nothing to do with business. Now she's quitting and Turner can at last confess his hunger and desire. We know you'll treasure this stirring romance from Patt.

In her new LOVESWEPT, Diane Pershing gives you a dangerously sexy hero who offers nothing but **SATISFACTION**, #615. An irresistibly wicked rebel, T. R. is every woman's dream, but Kate O'Brien has vowed never to fall for another heartbreaker. Still, how can she resist a man who warns her she'll be bored with a safe, predictable guy, then dares her to play with his fire? Diane tells this story with breathtaking passion.

Prepare to thrill to romance as you read Linda Warren's second LOVESWEPT, **SWEPT AWAY**, #616. Jake Marlow never intended to return to the family whale-watching business, but he smells sabotage in the air—and he has to consider every possible suspect, including Maria Santos, the exquisitely beautiful fleet manager. The sparks of desire between these two can probably set fire to the ocean! A powerful romance from a powerful storyteller.

Adrienne Staff returns to LOVESWEPT with **PLEASURE IN THE SAND**, #617. In this heart-stirring romance, Jody Conners's nightmare of getting lost at sea turns into a dream when she's rescued by movie star Eric Ransom. Years ago Hollywood's gorgeous bad boy had suddenly dropped out of the public eye, and when he takes Jody to his private island, she discovers only she has the power to coax him—and his guarded heart—out of hiding. Welcome back, Adrienne!

On sale this month from Bantam are three fabulous novels. Teresa Medeiros follows her bestselling **HEATHER**

AND VELVET with **ONCE AN ANGEL**, a captivating historical romance that sweeps from the wilds of an exotic paradise to the elegance of Victorian England. Emily Claire Scarborough sails halfway around the world to find Justin Connor, the man who had cheated her out of her inheritance—and is determined to make him pay with nothing less than his heart.

With **IN A ROGUE'S ARMS**, Virginia Lynn delivers an enchanting, passion-filled retelling of the beloved Robin Hood tale, set in Texas in the 1870s. When Cale Hardin robs Chloe Mitchell's carriage, she swears to take revenge . . . even as she finds herself succumbing to the fascination of this bold and brazen outlaw.

IN A ROGUE'S ARMS is the first book in Bantam's ONCE UPON A TIME romances—passionate historical romances inspired by beloved fairy tales, myths, and legends, penned by some of the finest romance authors writing today, and featuring the most beautiful front and stepback covers. Be sure to look for **PROMISE ME MAGIC** by Patricia Camden, inspired by "Puss in Boots," coming in the summer of 1993, and **CAPTURE THE NIGHT** by Geralyn Dawson, inspired by "Beauty and the Beast," coming in the late fall of 1993.

Favorite LOVESWEPT author Fran Baker makes a spectacular debut in FANFARE with **THE LADY AND THE CHAMP**, which Julie Garwood has already praised as "Unforgettable . . . a warm, wonderful knockout of a book." You'll cheer as Maureen Bryant and Jack Ryan risk anything—even Jack's high-stakes return to the ring—to fight for their chance at love.

Bantam/Doubleday/Dell welcomes Jane Feather with the Doubleday hardcover edition of **VIRTUE**. Set in Regency England, this highly sensual tale brings together a strong-willed beauty who makes her living at the gaming tables and the arrogant nobleman determined to best her with passion.

Happy reading!

With warmest wishes,

Nita Taublib
Associate Publisher
LOVESWEPT and FANFARE

Don't miss these fabulous
Bantam
Women's Fiction
titles
on sale in MARCH

ONCE AN ANGEL
by Teresa Medeiros

IN A ROGUE'S ARMS
by Virginia Brown
writing as Virginia Lynn

THE LADY AND THE CHAMP
by Fran Baker

In hardcover from Doubleday,
VIRTUE
by Jane Feather
author of
THE EAGLE AND THE DOVE

"From humor to adventure, poignancy to passion, tenderness to sensuality, Teresa Medeiros writes rare love stories to cherish." —*Romantic Times*

ONCE AN ANGEL
by Teresa Medeiros
author of HEATHER AND VELVET

From the enthralling Teresa Medeiros comes this irresistible new historical romance that ranges from the wilds of an exotic paradise to the elegance of Victorian England.

The last thing Justin Connor expected to find washed up on the wild shores of New Zealand was a young woman asleep on the sand, curled like a child beneath the moonlight. Though fiercely protective of the haven he had found on this island paradise, Justin was compelled to rescue this mysterious refugee, little realizing she would shatter his peace forever with her defiant courage, her vivid beauty, and the memories she stirred of a past best forgotten. . . .

Orphaned, cheated of her inheritance, Emily had sailed halfway around the world to find the man who had promised her father to take care of her—and instead had left her a charity case in an English boarding school. She never dreamed she'd be tossed by the pounding surf practically at his feet, or that she'd find him a disturbingly handsome recluse with the look of a pirate . . . and a disarming tenderness in his amber-flecked eyes. Confused by conflicting emotions, Emily was determined to make Justin pay for her years of loneliness with nothing less than his heart. . . .

Emily burrowed into the thin mattress, her mind tugging greedily at the blurred edges of sleep. She despised waking up. Despised the sleet tapping at the tiny attic window, the wash water frozen in her basin, the prospect of crawling down the steep stairs to teach French to wealthy little brats who didn't know their *demitasses* from their *derrières* and who teased her mercilessly because her dress was two years too small. Groaning, she fumbled for a pillow to pull over her head. Perhaps if she hid long enough, Tansy would come tapping on the door with a mug of steaming black coffee smuggled out from under Cook's bulbous nose.

Her groping search yielded no pillow. A new sensation crept over her, a feeling utterly delicious and so foreign to her gloomy attic that she wanted to weep at its beauty.

Warmth.

She slowly opened her eyes. The sun fanned tingling fingers across her face. She lay there, stunned, basking in its heat, enveloped in its healing rays. She closed her eyes against the dazzling shaft of light. When she opened them again, a twisted green face hung only an inch above her own, its pointed teeth bared in a ferocious grimace.

She shrieked and scrambled backward, groping for a weapon. Her fingers curled around the first blunt object they could find. As her back slammed into a wall, dust exploded, setting her off on a quaking chain of sneezes.

"Now look what you've done, Trinl. You've frightened the poor girl. I dare say she's never seen a savage before."

Emily wiped her streaming eyes. Now two faces were peering at her. One was still green, but the other was round and decidedly English. It was clicking its tongue and shaking its side-whiskers like a great overgrown hamster.

The fierce green face loomed nearer. "How do you do, miss? The sheer luminosity of your countenance beguiles me. I take extreme delight in welcoming you, our most charming breast."

The round face pinkened. Emily gaped. The savage's words had come rolling out in deep, resonant tones as if he'd just strolled from the hallowed corridors of Cambridge, his feathered cloak swinging around his shoulders. Emily realized his teeth were bared not in a snarl, but in a beaming smile. Nor was he entirely green. Deep furrows of jade had been tattooed in his honey-colored skin in elaborate curls and soaring wings.

A soft groan came out of the shadows. "Not breast, Trinl. *Guest.*"

She squinted into the corner, but the sunlight had blinded her. She could make out only a vague shape.

The tattooed man stretched out a hand. She recoiled and smacked it away. "I'll keep my breast to myself, thank you. I'm not a simpering ninny for some native Lothario to ravish."

The savage threw back his head. His musical laughter rocked the small hut.

"Did I say something amusing?" she asked the hamster. Her head was starting to pound and she was wishing even more desperately for that coffee.

"Oh, dear, I'm afraid so. You see—the Maori don't ravish their victims." He leaned forward and whispered, "They eat them."

Emily felt herself go the same color as the snorting native. She pressed herself to the wall. "Stay away from me. I'm warning the both of you. I wasn't kicked out of every girls' school in England for nothing." Emily disliked lying. She much preferred to embellish the truth.

She attacked the air with her makeshift weapon. The native danced backward. Narrowing her eyes in what she hoped was a menacing fashion, she said, "That's right. I know how to use this thing."

"What a comfort," came a dry voice from the corner. "If Penfeld ever decides to stop serving tea long enough to dust, you'll be of great service."

Emily glanced down to discover she was threatening a cannibal with a feather duster. Her cheeks burned.

A man unfolded himself from the shadows with lanky grace. He stepped into a beam of sunlight, tilting back a battered panama hat with one finger.

Their eyes met and Emily remembered everything. She remembered swimming until her arms and legs had turned leaden and her head bobbed under the water with each stroke. She remembered crawling onto the beach and collapsing in the warm sand. Then her memories hazed—a man's mouth melted tenderly into hers, his dark-lashed eyes the color of sunlight on honey.

Emily gazed up into those eyes. Their depths were a little sad, a trifle mocking. She couldn't tell if they mocked her or himself. She forced her gaze down from his, then wished she hadn't.

Her throat constricted. His physical presence was as daunting as a blow. She had never seen quite so much man. The sheer volume of his sun-bronzed skin both shocked and fascinated her. In London the men swathed themselves in layers of clothing from the points of their high starched collars to the tips of their polished shoes. Shaggy whiskers shielded any patch of skin that risked exposure.

But this man wore nothing but sheared-off dungarees that clung low on his narrow hips. The chiseled muscles of his chest and calves drank in the sunlight. To Emily's shocked eyes, he might as well have been naked.

Another unwelcome memory returned—damp sand clinging to her own bare skin. The pulse in her throat throbbed to mortified life. She glanced down to find herself wrapped in the voluminous folds of a man's frock coat. The sleeves hung far below her hands, nearly enveloping the duster.

"My man Penfeld was kind enough to lend you his coat."

The husky scratch of the stranger's voice sent shivers down her spine. An endearing lilt had been layered over his clipped

English, flavoring it with an exotic cadence. She had heard similar accents in Melbourne.

Disconcerted to find her thoughts read so neatly, she shot him a nasty look. A dazzling smile split the somber black of his stubbled chin. Dear Lord, the amiable wretch had kissed her! What other liberties had he taken while she lay in his embrace? Dropping the offensive duster, Emily buried her fists in the coat and hugged herself, fighting a sudden chill.

A Once Upon a Time Romance

IN A ROGUE'S ARMS
by Virginia Brown
writing as Virginia Lynn

From the bestselling author of LYON'S PRIZE and A TOUCH OF HEAVEN, this passion-filled retelling of "Robin Hood" is the story of a Texas outlaw and the pampered niece of his ruthless enemy.

One moment Chloe was lost in daydreams about her new Texas home; the next she was holding on for dear life as gunfire echoed and her uncle's carriage came rumbling to a halt! Before she could even draw a breath, the fair-haired beauty found herself on the ground. . . . and in the clutches of a bold and brazen outlaw known as "the Baron." Daring and dangerous, he took what he wanted from the wealthy, and now as she watched in helpless rage, he turned his hungry gaze upon her. . . .

For Cale Hardin, humiliation and empty pockets were a modest revenge for the crimes committed by Chloe's uncle, who made his money from the misery of others. Yet when the banker's niece came tumbling out of the carriage all spitting fury and white petticoats, Cale knew he at last had his foe where he wanted him. But what he didn't know, what he could never foresee, was his own reaction to the fair Chloe, for when he took her in his arms, he'd never want to let her go. . . .

"Kill me," she moaned, "I don't care, but I cannot get up and walk another step tonight. You'll have to drag my lifeless body somewhere to dispose of it. I can't move. I won't move. I hate you for being such a monster."

Cale sat his horse and watched her. Saddle leather creaked, and the wind sloughed through the trees with a swishing sound.

Chloe waited. Finally she lifted her head, and found him gazing at her with something close to sympathy. Then she thought she must be mistaken, because his expression was once more cold and remote. That brief impression, however, unnerved her.

Since she'd awakened to find him touching her, her feelings toward him had subtly altered. This smoky-eyed outlaw had somehow done much more than just touch her body. He'd awakened something inside her, some demon that pricked her at odd moments with the memory of how it had felt to be caressed intimately, to have his hands on her.

It was as if a stranger inhabited her body, some wicked creature without morals or pride and craved the sensuous feel of a man's hands. Disturbed by the unfamiliar emotions he provoked, Chloe struggled to recapture her original revulsion. He was a rogue and an outlaw and no decent woman could feel pleasure in his arms.

Chloe staggered to her feet, facing Cale and wondering why he kept staring at her with those bullet-gray eyes so unreadable in the shadows. Nothing showed on his face, no emotion, no reaction. It was unnerving. She stepped down from the porch.

"If you try to run," he said quietly, "I'll put the rope around you again. And it will stay there." His voice was flat and calm, but she knew he meant what he said.

God, he was so close, much too close for comfort. Why did he keep looking at her like that? Frozen, she could only stare up at him and wait.

Silence stretched tautly, and she couldn't look away. Dark shadows blurred around him as he swung down from his horse and crossed to her. One hand reached out to snag in her hair, tilting her head back so that she couldn't escape his gaze.

"You're poison, Chloe Mitchell," he muttered. "Sweet poison . . ."

There was only time for a gasp and grab at his arms before Cale was pushing her back against the porch. The edge caught her behind the knees, and when she went back in a graceless sprawl, he went with her. Taut muscles under her fingers felt like steel, inflexible and immovable.

Fear fluttered like a trapped bird in her chest. His hard, lean body felt like steel against hers, holding her down, his hands on each side of her head. He looked down at her for a long moment, his expression unreadable, his eyes veiled by his lashes. Chloe held to his arms as if drowning.

"Why are you doing this?" she asked when he pressed his mouth to her throat.

His head lifted. Satan's own eyes looked back at her, tarnished silver smoldering with sensuality beneath an inky brush of thick lashes. The breath caught in her throat, and something lurched through her. Excitement? Anticipation?

As her lips parted to protest, his mouth came over them. Then he was forcing her lips apart farther with his tongue, a heated invasion that thrust all thought of protest from her mind. A sound strangled in the back of her throat, surprise or excitement, or maybe a mix of the two.

His grip tightened on her, fingers spreading over her scalp as he held her head still for his tongue to explore her mouth. She moaned, unwilling participation. He seemed to like that as he explored more, drawing the breath from her lungs and sending small bursts of sensation licking along her stretched nerve ends.

When his head finally lifted, leaving her breathless and still and dazzled with reaction, his mouth flattened in a moody smile.

"I wanted you that first day I saw you."

"And now?" she got out, her voice a whisper of sound.

He released her and stood up, uncoiling his lead body into a straight line. He studied her gravely. "And now I have you."

"Unforgettable . . . a warm, wonderful knockout of a book." —Julie Garwood

THE LADY AND THE CHAMP
by Fran Baker

Walking into that fight gym was the hardest thing Maureen Bryant had ever done, but the painful memories of the father she barely knew vanished the instant she beheld the fighter in the ring. All sculpted muscles and sun-bronzed skin, Jack Ryan was the most gorgeous man she'd ever seen, a sleek Adonis whose powerful physique left her weak. But she knew better than to surrender her heart to another man who'd give her up without a second thought.

One look at the gym's new owner and Jack Ryan almost went down for the count. Yet he knew that beneath her elegant exterior, Sully's long-lost daughter couldn't have a heart. Sully had been the father that Jack had always needed, the only person who could have turned a troubled youth around. Now Jack was ready to do anything—even climb back into the ring for the biggest challenge of his life—to save Sully's gym from the woman who would let it die. But even as he put on the gloves, something told him the real fight would be in letting Maureen go. . . .

The man who climbed into the ring at that very same moment stopped her cold.

He wore a plastic headguard, black satin trunks, and nothing in between. His smooth, sun-bronzed neck flowed into shoulders that were about a yard wide and biceps that looked as round and firm as green apples. His red-gloved hands flashed like thunderbolts when he started shadowboxing, pummeling his invisible opponent with a furious flurry of rights and lefts.

Maureen abhorred violence, and she found no redeeming social value in blood sports of any kind. Standing ringside, though, she suddenly saw a brutal Renaissance beauty in the boxer's sculpted physique and athletic prowess, a beauty that was as frightening as it was fascinating to behold.

"He's all yours," said a gravelly voice just beside her.

Startled, she jumped, then spun to find she'd been joined by a balding little man with a big smile. She tilted her head, the better to hear him. "I beg your pardon?"

He pointed the unlit cigar he was carrying toward the muscular giant in the center ring. "I said, 'he's all yours.' "

"*Mine?*"

"You're Maureen, aren't you?"

Momentarily taken aback, she could only nod.

"Then you own his contract."

Now she shook her head. "But—"

"And he owes you a fight."

Puzzled, she swung her gaze back to the subject of this bizarre discussion. The commercial developer had mentioned something to the effect that she would probably have to buy out some old boxer's contract when she sold the gym. But the man in the ring looked to be in his prime.

"How old is he?" she asked, still grappling with this surprising news.

"Thirty-eight."

"That's not old!" Only three years older than she, in fact.

"It is for a fighter."

Maureen examined the boxer a little closer, looking for flaws. He hadn't gone to fat, as aging athletes are wont to do. To the contrary, his inverted triangle of a chest tapered to a trim waist and, judging from the way that black satin fabric draped itself over them, taut hips.

Nor did he seem to have "lost his legs," to quote a former Royals' baseball player whose trophy room she had recently redecorated. Quite the opposite, in fact. The boxer's powerful thighs and balustrade calves provided the perfect blend of balance and leverage as he danced backward and forward and sideways across the canvas in a pugilistic ballet that literally left her breathless.

She fanned her face, which suddenly felt warm, with her flat ivory clutch purse. Then she caught herself and, quickly dropping her hand, asked a question off the top of her head. "How much does he weigh?"

"One-ninety." Her sidekick hitched up his pants, and she was surprised he didn't strangle himself. "That's stripped, of course."

Her voice, when she managed to find it again, came out in a squeak. "Of course."

"You oughtta put another fifteen pounds on him before you fight him again."

Maureen pointedly ignored that piece of advice. "Has he ever won anything?"

"The Golden Gloves title."

"I thought that was for amateurs." Even as she said it, she wondered what hidden corner of her mind that tidbit had popped out of.

"It is."

"Well, I meant professionally."

"Seventeen KO's in eighteen fights."

"KO's?" She frowned, trying to put words to the strangely familiar term.

"Knockouts."

"Right." Now she smiled, inordinately pleased to have that clarified. "What happened in the eighteenth fight?"

For the first time since he'd walked up and started talking

to her, the man hesitated. He clamped the cold cigar between his teeth with fingers that were short and stubby and stained tobacco-brown. Then he chewed the stogie from one side of his mouth to the other before removing it and flicking the nonexistent ash onto the floor.

"Technical knockout," he said in a clipped tone.

She tipped her head inquiringly. "Which means?"

"The referee called the fight in the second round."

"Why?" She saw the reluctance in his pale blue eyes and realized she probably wasn't going to get an answer.

He proved her right when he gestured toward the ring and said with gravelly pride, "Now, was that sonofagun bred for battle, or what?"

Maureen responded more to the tone of his voice than to the visual impact of the boxer's shadow falling across the canvas like a double dare. "He's tall."

"Six foot one."

Her stomach fluttered as a gloved hand flashed through the air like heat lightning. "And he's certainly got long arms."

"Seventy-seven-inch reach."

A gruesome thought occurred to her. "He doesn't take steroids, does he?"

That earned a chuckle. "He's so anti-drug, he'd give an aspirin a headache."

"Well, he's—" she faltered slightly at the sight of the naked back—"extremely well-built."

"He works out every day, rain or shine."

"I see." Michelangelo's *David*, come to life and clad in black satin trunks—that's what she saw.

"Feel his biceps if you get a chance, and you'll find he's ninety-two percent muscle."

The man's suggestion brought Maureen back to earth with a bang. She had no intention of feeling the boxer's biceps. Or any other portion of his anatomy. But her palms—those traitors!—had a mind of their own. They just itched to feel the softness of his bare flesh, the heat and steel that rippled beneath.

Clutching her purse before her with both hands, she steered the discussion to safer ground. "What's his name?"

"Jack Ryan." No sooner had she filed that away for future reference than he added, "But Sully—God rest his soul—always carded him 'The Irish Terror.'"

She'd yet to get a good look at his face, but she could just picture the cauliflower ears and flattened nose—not to mention the ugly scars—that were the inevitable result of such a violent career. To top it off, a little voice inside her said, he was probably so punch-drunk that trying to talk business with him would be a waste of both her time and her breath.

If she had an ounce of sense, she thought, she'd walk out of here now and let her lawyer handle this. Yet she stood transfixed, awed by the beauty of the beast.

The reflection of the overhead light flickered across the rippling musculature of his torso. Sweat sheened his sun-baked skin and dampened the dark pelt of hair that bisected his massive chest. Veins mapped his biceps like the road to ruin for his hapless opponents.

He was the ultimate hard body. A lean, mean fighting machine, honed to perfection by years of rigorous training.

And to think, he was all hers . . .

You were entranced by *RAINBOW*,
captivated by *LAWLESS*,
and bedazzled by *LIGHTNING*.
Now get ready for...

Renegade

by

Patricia Potter

"One of the romance genre's greatest talents."
—*Romantic Times*

A new novel of romance and adventure...a passionate tale of a scoundrel who becomes a seeker of justice and the woman who tames his reckless heart.

When Rhys Redding is freed from a Confederate jail at the end of the Civil War by Susannah Fallon, he has no idea that she will demand that he take her across the lawless South to her home in Texas. As they traveled the scarred, burned-out land, they would feel the heat of passion's flame — but once they reached their destination, would Rhys take flight again...or would the man who insisted he had no soul realize that he'd found the keeper of his heart?

ON SALE IN APRIL

56199-5 $5.50/6.50 in Canada

❏ Please send me a copy of Patricia Potter's RENEGADE. I am enclosing $ 8.00 ($9.00 in Canada)—including $2.50 to cover postage and handling.
Send check or money order, no cash or C. O. D.'s please.
Mr./ Ms. _____
Address _____
City/ State/ Zip _____
Send order to: Bantam Books, Dept. FN100, 2451 S. Wolf Rd., Des Plaines, IL 60018
Please allow four to six weeks for delivery.
Prices and availability subject to change without notice.   FN100 - 4/93